Six-Guns at Solace

When Meg Thornton becomes caught up in a bank raid, she is horrified to discover that one of the raiders is her brother, Clay, who has been on the run since killing the barman in their home town. Clay has fallen in with the notorious Pike gang, and Eli Pike will kill Meg if he finds out she was a witness to the raid.

Can Clay extricate himself, and the girl he's fallen for, from the gang before Eli discovers there's a living witness to dispose of?

As an added complication, Meg is engaged to Solace's deputy sheriff, Tom Walsh, who has no idea that Meg has a brother, let alone one who is a fugitive from the law. In a possible showdown, Meg could end up with a dead brother or a dead fiancé – or both.

Six-Guns at Solace

John Davage

A Black Horse Western

ROBERT HALE

© John Davage 2018
First published in Great Britain 2018

ISBN 978-0-7198-2673-3

The Crowood Press
The Stable Block
Crowood Lane
Ramsbury
Marlborough
Wiltshire SN8 2HR

www.bhwesterns.com

Robert Hale is an imprint
of The Crowood Press

The right of John Davage to be identified as
author of this work has been asserted by him
in accordance with the Copyright, Designs and
Patents Act 1988

Typeset by
Derek Doyle & Associates, Shaw Heath
Printed and bound in Great Britain by
CPI Group (UK) Ltd, Croydon, CR0 4YY

PROLOGUE

He was just a kid, but a kid gone bad. It happened sometimes, they said later, after the unthinkable *had* happened.
But Mat Thornton's boy, to do a thing like that? Who
would have believed it? But there were witnesses, too many
for there to be any doubt. Sometimes it took just one
impulsive act, one crazy slip, to change the course of a
man's life, they said.

Clay was drunk, no question about it. It may have been
only ten in the morning, but the short, stocky sixteen-year-
old was already having trouble staying on his feet as he
started to make his way across the Lucky Dollar saloon,
heading for the stairs. His head was beginning to hurt, but
the stirring in his loins needed urgent attention. And he
knew precisely where to find pleasurable relief, and with
whom. Dolly, the plump little green-eyed, red-headed
saloon girl, knew exactly how to satisfy his carnal needs, as
he had discovered to his delight on more than one occasion.

5

A handful of onlookers watched him with some amusement as he put his foot on the first stair.

'Hold on there, Clay!' George Martin, the owner of Adam's Creek's only saloon, put a hand on Clay's shoulder to slow down the young man's progress. 'Now where d'you reckon you're going?'

'Mm? What?' Clay tried to focus on the other man.

George Martin turned and frowned at the barkeep. 'I've told you, Joe. No hard liquor for this kid. He can't hold it. Then, when he partakes of the pleasures of one of my girls, he gets rough, and they don't like it.'

The barkeep gave an apologetic shrug as he wiped a glass. 'Kid's kinda persuasive, George,' he said, choosing to omit the fact that Clay had slipped him a five-dollar tip to serve him – some of the money Clay had won in a poker game with three of the saloon's early drinkers. Clay may not have been able to hold his liquor but he was an accomplished poker player, and had been since about the age of fourteen. A *natural*, he had been called by one card sharp who had been passing through the town and had lost twenty dollars to the kid before getting his measure. Whether or not Clay was a natural *cheat* as well was open to question, but so far he'd never been challenged.

An inane smile spread across Clay's face as he looked at the saloon owner, and his words were slurred. 'Gonna get me some lovin', George.' He pointed to the top of the stairs. 'Gonna see Dolly for a. . . .'

His voice trailed off as he saw the expression on George's face.

George sighed. 'Nope, I reckon not, Clay,' he said. 'So you just turn yourself around and make your way home, there's a good kid. Maybe stop off at Cora's eating house for some good strong coffee on the way. Help to sober you up a mite.'

'Aw, hell . . .' Clay began.

'A fine, god-fearing man, your pa,' George said. 'Can't say I've ever known him take advantage of the female company here. And I don't reckon he'd thank me for allowing his son to make use of the – ' he looked round at the handful of other early drinkers in the bar and smiled – 'facilities as often as you do.'

There was a general chorus of chuckles, and Clay suddenly became aware that he was the centre of attention. And he didn't like it. He frowned, peered round at the grinning faces, and his own cheeks, already flushed from the drink, turned crimson with his growing humiliation. He pulled away from George's restraining grasp, marched across the room and, grabbing a man from the nearest table, backhanded him.

'Quit your laughin'!' he snarled.

The man fell back against the table, which gave under his weight, and he hit the floor amongst splintered wood and broken glass.

'That's enough!' shouted George, and made to grab Clay's arm.

He wasn't fast enough.

Clay reached out, pulled George's .45 from its holster and waved it in front of him.

'Anybody else think I'm a joke?' he yelled. He fired a shot into the ceiling, shattering a glass chandelier.

'Anybody?' He rubbed an old knife scar over his left eye, something he was inclined to do whenever he was agitated.

7

His glazed eyes circled the room. 'Come on, anybody else feel like laughin'?'

Smiles disappeared from faces, and George Martin backed away. An ominous silence fell over the room as some of the patrons edged their way towards the batwings, ready for a fast exit, whilst others froze in their chairs.

'Now take it easy, Clay,' George said, holding up a hand in front of him and breathing heavily. 'This is plain dumb. You ain't thinking straight. You know you ain't used to handling guns. Your pa's never let you . . .'

'Never mind my pa!' Clay snapped, trying to salvage some of his pride. 'Quit talkin' about my pa!' He glanced around with a glassy expression, the Peacemaker moving back and forth in front of him. It felt heavy in his hand, but it filled him with a sense of authority, a sense of power. 'My pa ain't here to say anythin'. So, anybody who reckons I can't handle a six-gun an' feels like testin' me – well, go ahead!'

For several moments nobody shifted. Then Clay heard a sudden movement behind him and swung round to see Joe, the barkeep, lifting a shotgun over the bar.

Later, Clay would have no recollection of firing the Peacemaker, no memory of pulling the trigger, but there was a sudden explosion – and a surprised expression appeared on the barkeep's face as a crimson stain spread across the front of his shirt.

Gasps of horror and astonishment echoed around the room as Clay stared down at the smoking gun in his hand as the barkeep's legs corkscrewed under him and he fell forwards on his face.

'Jeeze, I . . . I didn't mean . . .' Clay began, a mixture of dismay and terror filling his whole being. 'It went off before. . . .' He began rubbing his forehead violently.

A man vaulted over the bar and disappeared as he stooped over the barkeep's slumped form. After a moment he reappeared, his features pale. 'Joe's . . . dead,' he said.

A dozen pairs of accusing eyes turned towards Clay.

'It was an accident!' he yelled. 'For Chris' sakes, I didn't mean. . . .' His voice trailed away.

'Somebody fetch the sheriff,' George said, his words devoid of emotion as he looked at the sixteen-year-old.

'No!' Clay shouted, suddenly jerked back into life – suddenly sobered up by the turn of events. 'Nobody moves!'

His thoughts whirled and his head began to pound. He tried to think, suddenly confronted with the unpalatable options. What now? Lower his gun and face the consequences of a foolhardy albeit unlucky shooting? The result of which could be a hanging, or at the very least a life in Yuma prison?

Or go on the run?

Clay could feel his innards turning to liquid as he wrestled with the dilemma, but he tried to maintain some level of control – tried to steady his voice and his nerves.

'I'm leavin',' he said. 'An' . . . an' nobody moves or tries to come after me unless they want to end up like Joe. You listenin', all of you? Nobody moves, you hear?'

George Martin shook his head, a sad expression on his face. 'You thought this through, Clay?' he said. 'Right now it's just a case of a crazy, drunk kid accidentally shooting my barkeep. That's all it is. But leave here now, and you're a killer on the run, the target of posses and bounty

9

hunters. You want that? Now, let me get the sheriff and try to explain. Maybe I can . . .'

'No!' Clay cut in. 'I ain't riskin' jail, or worse still, a hangin' . . .'

George shrugged. 'I guess it's your decision, kid. But it's a bad one.'

'That's right, it's my decision,' Clay said, swaying on his feet. 'So everybody stays 'xactly where they are!'

He began backing away towards the batwings, his heart-beat thumping in his ears, beads of sweat prickling his forehead. Those men who had moved nearer the doors eased back to allow Clay through, none prepared to challenge him. Faces watched him – shocked, confused faces, staring at this *kid* who'd suddenly turned killer. Everybody knew he was wild, getting into fights, tom-catting with saloon girls, but *killing*?

Clay made it into the street. Once outside, he stuffed the six-gun into his belt and ran for his horse. Pulling himself into the saddle, he glanced up and down the street. It was surprisingly empty, the town almost too quiet for that time of day. The single shot seemed to have done little to disturb the lethargy of the mid-morning in the little town. He glanced back at the saloon. Nobody was attempting to follow him.

Seconds later, he was riding away like a man pursued by the devil.

'That brother of yours should've been back an hour ago.'

Matthew Thornton came into the kitchen of the small farmhouse, five miles north of the town of Adam's Creek. The bleached sun behind his thin, stooped figure threw

10

his shadow across the doorway. Lines of anxiety were etched into his forehead, and there was a bone-weary look of exasperation in his pale blue eyes. He was a tall, spare man, not an ounce of fat on his work-ravaged body. Fifty years old, but with the look of a man ten years older. Grey stubble, grey hair, grey pallor. Matthew Thornton knew he was a dying man, it hadn't needed Doc Brown to tell him that. Even so, he greeted each day with a mixture of hope and despair where his wayward son was concerned.

'Darn it, Meg,' he said. 'He only had to pick up a few things from the mercantile and come straight home. Can't I even trust him to do a simple thing like that?'

His seventeen-year-old daughter sighed and put down the washcloth she'd been using at the sink. She dried her hands on her apron before untying it and dropping it on to a chair.

'I'll go and look for him, Pa,' she said. 'Don't worry. You sit awhile, you're tired. There's fresh coffee in the pot.'

Matthew sat down at the table and shook his head despairingly. He picked up the coffee pot to pour some of the steaming liquid into a mug but seemed to lose interest in it at the last minute, replacing it on the table.

'Chances are he'll be in the Lucky Dollar, playing poker with a bunch of the no-hopers who congregate there as soon as the place is open. Probably using the money I gave him for the mercantile as a stake. I've begged him to stay out of that place, but he stopped doing what I asked a long time ago.'

'It's not your fault, Pa,' Meg said.

'Maybe I should go,' he said, breathing hard. 'I . . . I just don't like you going into that place, Meg. Some of the

11

women are . . . well. . . .'

'I know what some of the unfortunate women there have to do, Pa, I'm not a child.' Meg smiled and put an arm round his shoulder. 'I'll be fine, don't worry.' She was a tall girl with the same chestnut-coloured hair and green eyes of her dead mother. Sometimes she could see her father looking at her with moist eyes, and she knew that her growing likeness to his wife moved him deeply.

He was a virtuous, upright man of high morals, and he had tried to bring up his two children with similar values during the nine years since his wife had died of the fever. But now, his own health failing, Meg knew he was near to conceding defeat with his son.

Clay was always arguing and brawling and getting into fist fights – and on one memorable occasion a year back, had got himself into a knife fight which had left its mark on his forehead in a sickle-moon-shaped scar. Not that he had learned his lesson.

She poured her father a cup of coffee. 'Just take it easy, Pa,' she said.

He nodded. 'I'll be OK.' He put a hand on her arm. 'Listen, Meg. If . . . when anything happens to me. . . .'

'Pa!' Meg tried to stop him, but he shook his head.

'Let me finish, girl. You're not stupid, you know I'm dying. And when I'm gone, I want you to go and live with your ma's sister and her husband in Solace. They know the . . . situation with me. I wrote them some time back. They've said they'd be plum proud to have you live with them, maybe help out at the mercantile which your Uncle Chester owns.' He frowned. 'Not sure how they'd feel about taking on Clay, but maybe . . .' His voice trailed off.

Meg moved towards the door. 'Stop worrying, Pa. Things will take care of themselves. Just rest now. I'll take the buckboard. I shan't be long.'

'All right, but take care,' Matthew said, his voice drained to a near whisper. 'Get George Martin to give you a hand with the young varmint if necessary. Why George lets Clay drink there when I've begged him to turn the boy away I don't know.'

'Mr Martin may not be there,' Meg said. 'And you know how persuasive my little brother can be.'

'That's true,' Matthew agreed, ruefully. 'He could sweet talk the barkeep round. Joe Brewer's a soft touch.'

She smoothed down the front of her jeans, took a Stetson from a hook by the door, and stepped out into the late morning sun.

Already the heat was building. By noon the humidity would drench her with sweat. A thunderstorm was needed, but the sky was cloudless, the ground dry and hard. Minutes later, sitting straight-backed on the seat of the buckboard, she set off on the narrow twisting trail that led to town.

Meg was three miles from Adam's Creek when she saw a cloud of dust, signalling the approach of a fast-moving rider.

'Clay,' she muttered to herself. 'And in a hurry. Well, at least he's got the good sense to realize he's late back.'

But minutes later, as he brought his horse to a halt alongside the buckboard, she could see from the expression on his face that something was badly wrong.

'Clay?' she said. 'What is it?'

The words tumbled from his mouth as he tried to

13

explain what had happened at the saloon. 'It was an accident, Meg! Jeeze, I didn't mean to . . . I mean everythin' happened so fast, an'. . . .'

'Whoa! Slow down,' Meg said. 'What happened so fast?'

'The gun – it just went off in my hand,' Clay said.

'*Gun!*' Meg felt the blood drain from her face.

'It wasn't meant . . . I . . . he's dead, Meg, Jeeze, he's dead!'

'Who? Who's dead? Clay, I don't understand.' Meg put a hand on his arm, panic rising in her breast. 'Just calm down and tell me exactly what happened.'

Clay swallowed and began to rub the knife scar on his forehead. 'Joe Brewer, the barkeep,' he said. 'I . . . I killed him.'

It was only then that Meg noticed the six-gun stuffed into the waistband of his jeans. 'Wh-where did you get . . . that?' Her brother never carried a six-gun, she knew that.

'It's George Martin's gun,' he said. 'I took it from him.' He looked over his shoulder, raw panic in his eyes. 'Meg, I've got to get away. They'll be formin' a posse by now. They'll be comin' after me.'

'No!' Meg said. 'You mustn't! You can't run away from this, Clay. For once in your life you've got to stay and face the consequences. Pa will help you to straighten things out, and. . . .'

'I ain't stayin', Meg,' he cut in. 'I ain't gonna be hanged or go to jail. I just ain't.'

'You're going to live the life of a fugitive?' Meg said. 'For the next I-don't-know-how-many years? But that's crazy!'

'There ain't no alternative.'

14

Meg tried to collect her thoughts, seeing that her brother was determined to take his chances. 'But . . . do you have money?'

He nodded. 'I've got the money Pa gave me for the things from the mercantile, plus what I won at cards. Best part of forty dollars. Guess I'll have to use that to tide me over.'

'But, Clay, I still don't understand what happened at the saloon.'

'You'll find out soon enough,' he replied. 'Word'll get around faster than a prairie fire.' He looked over his shoulder again, a bleak expression on his face. 'I've got to go.' He reached across and kissed his sister on the cheek. 'Tell Pa . . . I'm sorry. Sorry for everythin'. . . .'

With that, he swung his horse around and galloped away before she could reply.

It would be more than two years before Meg saw her brother again. And by that time, and in those particular circumstances, she would wish that she hadn't.

CHAPTER ONE

Becky Garrod shifted uncomfortably in the corner seat of the stagecoach, conscious of the overweight body of the woman sitting next to her as the latter's fleshy thigh pressed against Becky's leg. Then there was the June heat. Her underclothes were sticking to her and she could feel the prickles of sweat on her forehead, in spite of leaning out of the window from time to time to catch what little air there was.

She glanced around at the rest of her fellow passengers. There was the husband of Fat Thighs sitting the other side of his wife. In a round of introductions at the start of the journey, they had introduced themselves as Mr and Mrs Hector Pratt. But he'd had little or nothing to say during the fifty or so miles since they had left Becky's home town of Solace. He seemed an anxious little man in a shiny too-tight dark suit and a string tie. He clutched a black bowler in his hands, revolving it nervously in his fingers.

The man in the seat opposite Becky was in his forties, she guessed. A gambler, maybe? 'Cal Farrow,' he'd introduced himself as. He wore a white alpaca suit and a planter's hat, and had a way of looking at Becky as if – well, as if he knew what she looked like in her chemise! Becky felt a wicked yet pleasurable thrill at the thought.

Next to him was the drummer. ('Sidney Mason, that's me.') A skinny little runt with frayed cuffs to his jacket and holes in the soles of his shoes, and a tired look that indicated too many years on the road. Probably nearing fifty, Becky guessed.

Jeeze, what a bunch, she thought, and silently cursed her pa for sending her on this miserable journey. And all because she'd been a little wild and – all right – maybe a little over-friendly with some of the young men in Solace. But was that any reason to pack her off to stay with some distant relatives up north she didn't know, cousins of her pa whom she'd never met?

'Just for a few months, my girl,' he'd said, exasperation in his voice. 'Maybe they can knock some ladylike manners and some good sense into you. "Fast Missy", that's what the church-going ladies of Solace call you, and they're right. Well, things have got to change.'

'Fast Missy!' Becky smiled to herself as she thought of the church-going old biddies. Bet the dried-up old sticks were just envious, if truth were told. When was the last time any young hombre had whistled at them or pinched *their* behinds!

Still, maybe it was a good time to get out of Solace. 'What's more, it'll give time for folks to forget all about you and Tom Walsh and that little embarrassing episode,' her pa had said – and maybe he was right.

Tom Walsh. Becky felt a pang of regret as she thought about the good-looking young man. For a while, and

17

seemingly much to her pa's relief, it had looked like she might have hooked herself a husband in the town's young deputy. But a year ago a nineteen-year-old girl (two whole years younger than Becky!) from someplace a hundred odd miles away called Adam's Creek had turned up. She had come to live with the Greens at the mercantile (relatives, apparently) after the death of her father. And all of a sudden, Tom Walsh's interest in Becky's more obvious charms had shifted to the pretty young incomer's more subtle allure. Like a bee drawn to a honeypot, he'd been. And now, dammit, the two of them were engaged to be married, leaving Becky the laughing stock of her female contemporaries in Solace.

So, yes, maybe it had been a good time to get out of Solace.

Becky sighed and stared out of the window at the barren landscape of sagebrush and a group of rocky outcrops. Excitement, that's what she craved. A dark-haired handsome man to carry her off and show her a good time. Maybe spiced up with a smidgen of danger, even! Yes, that's what she needed – a little *danger*. She chuckled to herself, attracting the attention of at least one of her fellow passengers.

'Something amusing you, missy?' the Pratt woman asked, looking down her nose at Becky.

'Yeah, you are,' Becky retorted, suddenly feeling bold. 'Loosen your girdle a mite an' I reckon you could get a job as the Fat Lady in a carnival show.'

Cal Farrow stifled a laugh, but the outraged reply that the woman was about to hurl at Becky was cut short by the stage's sudden quickening of pace, and a yell from the driver as he wielded his whip on the horses.

'What the hell. . . ?' Farrow began.

Suddenly the sound of gunfire crackled around them, and bullets zinged off the sides of the stage. There was a return volley from the shotgun rider sitting next to the stage driver, followed by a grunt as he was hit by one or more of the outlaws' bullets and the sound of him falling sideways into the dust.

'Get down!' yelled the drummer, and threw himself on to the floor as the stage began to sway from side to side.

'Owlhoots!' Farrow drew a derringer from under his jacket. 'Guess we're about to be held up.' He continued to peer out of the window, as if calculating the odds. After a moment, he slipped the gun back under his coat. 'Six of them. Don't reckon our chances,' he said. 'Best reconcile ourselves to losing some of our valuables if we're to stay alive. No time to be heroes, folks.'

The Pratts clung together in their seat like a pair of Siamese twins as Becky felt herself being pulled to the floor by Farrow, seconds before a bullet whizzed through the window, embedding itself into the back of the seat where she'd been sitting.

'Sweet Jesus!' she said. What was it she had been craving? Excitement? *I should be more careful what I wish for*, she thought.

In spite of the pace the driver had managed to urge the horses to pick up, the outlaws were gradually overhauling the stage. Moments later they were alongside it, three on either side.

'Pull over!' Becky heard one of them yell at the driver. 'Or you're dead meat!'

The driver, who had no wish to meet the same fate as his shotgun rider, did as he was bidden, hauling the stage to a halt in a haze of dust.

'Now climb over the top and toss down the bags. Fast!'

'OK, OK!' The driver scrambled across the roof of the stage and began to untie the straps holding the passengers' baggage at the rear of the vehicle.

The masked riders circled the stage. Several dismounted and began ripping open the bags and tossing the contents of each on to the ground, searching for anything worth taking. Another pulled open the stage door with one hand, waving a six-gun with the other. 'Get out, all of you!' he yelled at those inside. 'An' toss any weapons out ahead of you.'

The drummer was the first to scramble out, hands in the air. 'I . . . I'm just a drummer, an' I ain't carrying any guns an' no money to speak of, m-mister. Don't shoot.'

Next the nervous Mr Pratt emerged ahead of his wife; he turned to take her arm. She followed, for once speechless. Once outside, the pair of them placed their hands on their heads. 'We have no valuables,' Pratt said to the riders at large, 'other than my pocket watch and a few dollars. Take those and don't hurt us.'

'Shut your mouth an' line up with the drummer,' one of the dismounted outlaws told him, then looked back at the open stagecoach door as Becky stepped out into the hot sun.

'Well, lookee here, Boss,' he said, chuckling. 'Reckon we've got ourselves a pretty little bonus!'

A rider on a large black stallion, responding to the word 'boss', edged his mount forwards to within a couple of yards of Becky. Then, taking his time and assessing his prize, he dismounted and walked over to her. At the same moment Cal Farrow tossed out his weapon and stepped from the stage with his hands in the air.

'We're no heroes, mister,' he said. 'Just take it easy.'

The apparent boss of the outfit gave him a cold stare. 'Get in line an' button your lip,' he said. He turned back to Becky, took hold of her arm and drew her alongside him, away from the other passengers. He took her chin in his hand and pulled her closer to his face. Becky could smell his sour breath. She almost gagged.

'You're journey ends here, darlin'. You're comin' with me,' he told her.

Becky was too frightened to speak. She could feel a dampness in her drawers and her heart was pounding like a jackhammer. Yet at the same time, she recognized a stirring within her that was a mixture of fear and . . . there was that word again: *excitement?*

'Hey, leave her! You can't. . . !' Farrow began, stepping forwards.

The boss man turned, unleashed his six-gun from its holster and fired – all in one swift movement. The bullet took Farrow in the centre of his chest before he fell backwards into the dust.

The Pratt woman began whimpering and her husband drew her closer to him. 'Dear God,' he began. 'What kind of animals are. . . ?' – then whelped like a whipped dog as the back of the masked man's hand smashed across his face, loosening his front teeth and sending a trickle of blood from his mouth.

'You were told to keep quiet,' the boss man said. 'Now,

you and the drummer empty your pockets.' He glanced at Pratt's wife. 'An' woman, if'n you've got anythin' hidden in your clothin', now's the time to hand it over, lessen you want one of my cahoots to strip you an' check.'

He gripped Becky's arm and drew her across to his horse. He pulled her up on to the animal so that she was sitting astride in front of him, skirt bunched up around her waist, his hand firmly around her middle.

Two of the outlaws went through the luggage, removing cash, trinkets and other valuables. Another of the men relieved the Pratts and the drummer of their cash, watches and jewellery. Pratt was found to be concealing a money belt under his shirt.

'Just "a few dollars", eh?' the outlaw frisking him grabbed him. 'Liar!'

And he gave Pratt a second backhander, loosening more of the little man's teeth.

Fifteen minutes later the six outlaws rode away, but not before smashing two wheels of the stagecoach and scattering the horses. The driver and his three remaining passengers stood in a bewildered group under the hot sun, their ransacked baggage strewn around them.

CHAPTER TWO

Clay could *feel* the intensity of the man's stare, although he avoided looking in the hombre's direction. The man was sitting on a stool at the bar across the other side of the saloon, a whiskey in his hand and a half-smile on his face. He was playing solitaire on the bar top.

He had been watching Clay for the past fifteen minutes. Over the past two years Clay had learned to suspect any unasked-for attention paid to him by strangers. A stranger who might have seen his youthful face on a law dodger. The fact that he'd grown a stubbly beard and allowed his hair to get to near shoulder length, may not have been a sufficient disguise for some lawman or bounty hunter with a sharp eye. Or even the fact that this particular saloon in this particular town – Weslake – was close on two hundred miles from Adam's Creek. He had been going under the name of Chet Adams since he'd been on the run, but maybe none of these things had been enough. So a curious stranger always rang an alarm bell in Clay's head.

Maybe it was time to move on again, to another town. He sighed. More bumming drinks, cheating at cards, cleaning out livery stables or working as a swamper. Nickles and dimes jobs. Living hand to mouth and always looking over his shoulder. What he needed was a way of making some real money. Enough to get him to Canada, maybe.

Maybe, maybe, maybe. Hell, his whole life was a succession of maybes these days!

'You plannin' on dealin' those cards anytime soon, kid?' The old grizzled guy sitting across the table from Clay was getting impatient. 'Reckon you've been shufflin' 'em for the best part of five minutes now.'

'OK, OK!' Clay turned his attention to the game of poker, aware of the hostile gazes of the guy's two younger companions. Clay sensed that getting out of this game was not going to be easy, particularly as he had benefited from a lucky streak. But it had to be done. The man at the bar was worrying him and the sooner he was out of this place the better. 'Matter of fact though,' he said, adopting a casual tone, 'it's time I made a move to go.' He placed the pack of cards on the table. 'Thanks for the game, fellahs. Let me buy y'all a drink before. . . .'

'Now hold on, kid,' the grizzled guy said. 'You ain't goin' anyplace until we've had a chance to get some of our money back.' As if to emphasize the point, he placed a hand on the sawn-off shotgun that had sat in his lap throughout the game.

'That's right,' agreed on of his compatriots. 'Be right *unfriendly* of you to walk away now.'

Clay tried to figure the odds. Could he get a hand to his .45 before the grizzled old man triggered the sawn-off shotgun.

As it turned out, he was saved having to make a decision. It was at that moment the man at the bar chose to put down the pack of cards he'd been playing with and move off from his stool.

He ambled over to Clay's table and stood at Clay's shoulder, looking from one to the other of the three men. 'Mornin' fellahs.' His voice was a soft drawl which could not disguise an undertone of menace. 'Everythin' OK?'

Clay was aware of a shift in the atmosphere.

'M-mornin', Mr Riggens,' the old grizzled guy said, quickly moving his hand away from his lap. 'Sure, sure.' His two fellow card players avoided the eye of the newcomer.

'Some sort of problem here?' Riggens enquired.

'No problem, Mr Riggens. The kid was plannin' to leave afore we had a chance to win back a few of the dollars he took off us, that's all.'

'He win them fair and square?' Riggens asked.

'Well, yes. . . .'

'Then I reckon he can choose to leave whenever he wishes, don't you?'

Riggens stared at each of the three men in turn, challenging them to argue. None did.

'You reckoning on staying in Weslake, kid?' Riggens asked, turning his attention to Clay.

Clay shook his head. 'Just passin' through.'

'Been helpin' out here for a coupla days, Ray,' the barkeep called across. 'Swamper, part-time barman.'

'That so, Harry?' Riggens said without looking away from Clay. 'You lookin' for somethin' better, kid? Maybe I can help.'

'Well, I guess . . .' Clay hesitated. He was quickly coming to the conclusion that the kind of work this hombre had to offer would put him on the wrong side of the law. But what the hell, he was already in that precarious position, wasn't he? So what was there to lose? Besides, whatever the work was, it would beat cleaning up bar slops.

'Let me buy you a drink while you consider it . . . *Clay*,' Riggens said.

Clay felt his innards do a somersault. 'The name's Chet,' he said, dry-mouthed all of a sudden. 'Chet Adams.'

'Oh, sure,' Riggens said. 'Well let's find another table and have a talk, Chet.'

Clay followed Riggens over to a corner table, his thoughts whirling.

How did this guy know his real name? Was he a bounty hunter? But, no. The three card players knew him, so he had to be local to Weslake, didn't he?

One thing was certain. The three hadn't wanted to argue with him. Something about the man had unnerved them. And Clay was beginning to feel the same way.

When they were seated, Riggens motioned to the barkeep and moments later a bottle of whiskey and two glasses appeared on the table. Riggens poured two shots, then pushed one glass across to Clay.

'Thing is . . . Clay,' Riggens said. 'I pay special attention to any law dodgers I come across.' He gave a crooked grin. 'For one thing, there's always a chance I'll see a picture of myself.' He tossed back the shot of whiskey and poured himself another.

Clay's remained untouched.

'And the thing is,' Riggens resumed, 'I've a good

memory for faces.' He lowered his voice and leaned across the table. 'Even when that face has grown a beard and let its hair grow down over his neck. Got me . . . *Clay*?'

Clay steadied his hand sufficient to pick up his glass. He swallowed a mouthful of red-eye. 'What d'you want, mister?' he said.

'To do you a favour,' Riggens said. 'A chance to make some real money.'

'Why me?' Clay said.

'I've been watchin' you, an' I judge you to be the kinda kid who might not be afraid of usin' a gun.' He glanced around to ensure nobody was paying them any attention. The three card players had upped and left, and there was only the barkeep, and he was polishing glasses that didn't need polishing. 'You ever heard of the Pike Gang, kid?'

A cold hand seemed to crawl up Clay's spine. 'Yeah,' he said after a moment. 'Yeah, I've heard of then.'

'Thing is,' Riggens said. 'Somebody like you, who ain't fussy about usin' a gun on a fellah. . . .'

'I only ever killed one man, and it was an accident,' Clay put in quickly.

'Yeah, well, it put you on the wrong side of the law,' Riggens chuckled. 'So that makes us sorta kinfolk, kid. An' we – the gang – are a mite short-handed after a couple of our bunch decided to high-tail it down south. Seems they wanted to set up on their own an' decided, sensibly, not to go into competition with Eli and Silas Pike. 'Cause that would have been fatal, know what I mean?'

Clay nodded. 'Look, I appreciate the offer, Mr Riggens, but I ain't sure . . .' he began.

Riggens' expression hardened. He put a hand across

27

the table and took hold of Clay's wrist in a vice-like grip, making Clay cry out. 'It don't pay to refuse a proposition like this, kid, 'specially when a word to our local lawman could see you headin' for a hangman's noose.'

'OK, OK!' Clay gasped. 'I . . . I do need work. So, yeah, OK.'

Riggens smiled. 'Good thinkin', kid. Get your things together an' be ready to leave in half an hour.'

And so began Clay Thornton's association with one of the most ruthless and brutal gangs in the West.

CHAPTER THREE

By the time they were ten miles outside of Weslake, the five riders had pulled down the neckerchiefs that had masked the lower halves of their faces, and slowed their horses to a canter: Eli Pike, his brother Silas, Ray Riggens, Nate Morgan, and the kid, Chet Adams.

Becky watched them approaching as she stood in the shade of the porch of the Lazy O ranch house, out of the blistering mid-day sun. She had been standing, waiting for the men for some time and her facial expression was one of anxiety as she tried to assess their mood as they drew closer. She said a silent prayer that all had gone according to plan and that Eli's temper would have calmed since the time he'd left earlier. She had become used to his violent mood swings, but she could read nothing from the expressions on the faces of Eli or the others.

If any of her former friends in Solace could have seen her now, they would barely have recognized her. Whatever spirit for life, whatever sense of fun and daring Becky had once possessed, Eli had been beaten out of her, leaving a

cowed, subservient girl who cringed at the slightest movement of his hand.

Eli Pike was a big, muscular man, with a mop of shiny
black hair that reached almost to his shoulders, and a
black beard that hid two-thirds of his face.

Silas had his brother's swarthy good looks, but they
were marred by a lazy eye and cheeks pocked by eczema.
He was shorter, but built in much the same way as Eli. He
sported a drooping moustache above a stubbled chin. His
good eye had a mean glint in it, and for some unexplained
reason his mouth was always twisted into a humourless half
smile, except when he was angry.

Morgan always stood out from the others due to the
long brown riding duster that he wore no matter what the
heat, together with his broad-brimmed black hat. He was
tall and lean with a hooked nose like the beak of an eagle,
and whenever he looked at you, his eyes seemed to pene-
trate your soul. Becky did her best to stay out of his way.

Ray Riggens, the oldest of the bunch, was the cool, calm
one, his face registering nothing, but his eyes missing little
that happened around him. He had introduced Chet
Adams – whom everyone called the kid – and, in his own
fashion, had looked out for him.

Adams had been with the gang little more than a few
months, arriving less than a month after the stage hold-up
when Becky herself had been taken by Eli. But today was
the first time Eli had tested the kid's mettle by taking him
on a stage hold-up. Now he trailed behind the others, as
though acknowledging his place in the gang's hierarchy.
He was a good-looking boy, Becky thought, apart from the
scar over his left eye and the wispy beard he refused to

shave off.

The Lazy O wasn't a working ranch, and made no pretence of being one. Most of the land, apart from that adjacent to the two-storey ranch house, bunkhouse and corral, had been sold off soon after Eli and his brother Silas had taken over the place a year earlier, having terrorized and driven out the previous owner and his wife and daughter.

The house itself was in need of some serious repairs, but Eli and his brother showed no inclination to do anything about them. It was a temporary home (some folk in the nearby town of Weslake referred to it as 'Pike's hideout') for Eli and his gang. It served a purpose, nothing more.

Already Eli was talking about moving out of the territory. Some of the townsfolk were starting to get uncooperative, even troublesome, he had told Becky. Not Cord Lewis, of course, Weslake's sheriff. Cord did as he was damn well told. But some of the others, that tiresome mayor for example, and the members of the town council, were getting to be a burr in Eli's britches.

The stage they had robbed that morning lay abandoned some twenty miles north of Weslake. When they had left it an hour or so ago, the driver and shotgun rider lay dead in the dust, the team of six horses were unhitched and scattered, and the four passengers were mourning the loss of their money and valuables, and scratching their heads wondering how they were going to finish their journey.

Becky came down off the porch as Eli dismounted his horse.

'Everthin' go OK, Eli?' she asked, a nervous edge to her voice. She was five foot tall and had been pert and pretty six months ago. Now her looks had faded. There were lines of anxiety on her face, and a purple bruise on the side of her neck. This was only the latest evidence of Eli's rough treatment. Other, slowly fading bruises were covered by her clothing. She had learned not to complain.

He stared at her momentarily, then said, 'Yeah, it went OK.' He smacked his lips. 'I could use a drink though.'

Becky pasted a smile on her face. 'Sure, Eli. I'll get you . . .' she began.

Eli waved away her reply, took her arm and led her inside the ranch house. Wincing at the tightness of his grip, she made no other reference to what he and the others had been doing that morning, even though she knew about the hold-up, having heard snatches of their conversation when they were planning it. Eli preferred to believe she knew nothing, and she was happy to keep it that way.

For some reason any law-breaking activity always aroused his sexual appetite as well as his thirst. Today, she realized with a sinking feeling, was no different. After grabbing a bottle of whisky en route, he propelled her towards the stairs and their bedroom.

Clay Thornton/Chet Adams watched them as he and the others entered the ranch house. 'Bastard!' he muttered under his breath.

Even though he had been part of the gang for just a few months, for some weeks now he had been conscious of his own growing feelings towards Becky. It was a protective-ness that was rapidly developing into a fondness, or even

32

something more. Consequently, the bitterness and resentment he felt at Eli's assumed rights of possession burned his insides, not least because he felt helpless to do anything about it.

To witness the cruelty with which the older man treated the girl and do nothing about it was an exercise in self-control on Clay's part. His whole being wanted to strike out – even *kill* – the gang leader whenever the latter yelled at her or raised a hand to her. And the images that seared his imagination as he thought about what Eli probably demanded of her in the bedroom drove him crazy.

For now, though, he fought down the urge to mount the stairs and drag her away from the older man. Instead, he joined the three others as they emptied the contents of their saddle-bags on to the pine table in the centre of the room. A mixture of banknotes, coins and jewellery spewed out, some spilling on to the ranch-house floor.

Clay watched the others' faces for their reactions. The take was clearly less than they'd hoped for. Silas swore as he looked over the spoils, scowling and pushing a hand through his thick black hair.

'Jeeze, look it at! Eli ain't gonna be happy with that measly haul,' he said.

Nate Morgan sniffed and said nothing. The skinny, hook-nosed thirty-year-old rarely spoke. But his reticence belied his mean and violent temper, and even in the short period he had been with the gang, Clay had learned to avoid him much of the time.

Ray Riggens, tall and bald except for a few sparse greying hairs, shrugged and eased himself into a chair, stretching his long legs out in front of him. 'There'll be another day,' he muttered.

Silas glared at him. 'That all you can say? Don't you give a damn?'

Ray shrugged again. 'No sense cryin' over it, is there?'

'So maybe you'll forgo your share, an' we'll make it a four-way split instead of five.' Silas grinned nastily. 'Maybe we should cut you out, Ray, seein' as you're so goddamned indifferent.'

Ray gave him a cold stare, and as if to make a point, laid his hand over the holster holding his six-gun. 'Don't even think of ever doin' that, Silas,' he said quietly.

Anger flared in Silas' good eye, and the hatred that Clay had sensed existed between the two men became evident before Silas looked away.

The other three retreated to individual chairs and sank down into them. Ray and Silas began to drink steadily, and within less than half an hour both were sleeping. Nate took a knife from the sheath he kept inside his right boot and became absorbed in whittling a piece of wood, paring each slice with a fierce concentration.

Clay observed them, ruefully reflecting his association with the Pike gang and what they expected of him. At first it had been simple things, like looking after the horses outside the bank or the mining office whilst the others robbed it. But today it had meant taking a full part in the stage hold-up to earn his share of the takings. And even though it had only entailed sitting on his horse and pointing his Winchester at the stage driver, it had been terrifying.

But on the good side, in the time he'd been with the gang, Clay had never had so much money – never *seen* so much money. A lot better than the chancy, and sometimes just as dangerous, occupation of cheating at cards!

But there was an extra price to pay, and Clay paid it every time he looked at the fear and shame in Becky's eyes, and suffered the gut-wrenching feeling that went with seeing her at Eli Pike's side.

CHAPTER FOUR

'You OK, kid? You look like you want to kill someone!'

Ray's voice seemed to come from nowhere, rousing Clay from his reveries.

'Wh. . . what. . . ?' Clay started. 'Oh, yeah, sure. I'm OK.'

Eli and Becky had come down from upstairs. Becky had the usual whipped look about her that cut Clay to the quick. He stared at her, but she wouldn't meet his eyes, looking at the floor instead. Did she know he felt about her? It was a question he asked himself almost daily without knowing the answer.

Eli took one look at the spread of notes, coins, watches and jewellery on the table, cursed loudly and kicked Silas awake.

'Is that it?' Eli yelled. 'Shee-*it*!'

Silas awoke with a start, while Ray roused himself more slowly. Both men exchanged glances before looking at the irate Eli. Nate glanced up, then went back to his whittling, seemingly unconcerned.

'Yeah, that's it, Eli,' Silas said, rubbing sleep from his

eyes. 'Ain't much, is it?' He looked apologetic, as though he was personally to blame for the deficit.

'No, it damn well ain't! So it's just as well we can expect more from the next job.' Eli fingered a wad of notes before throwing them back on the table in disgust. 'At least we can rely on the take bein' a whole lot bigger.'

Clay sat up straight, suddenly curious. 'What job is that, Eli?' he asked. He'd heard nothing about another hold-up or raid.

Eli grinned at him. 'You'll find out soon enough, kid,' he said. 'You did good today. Anyways, right now I want you to take the buckboard an' drive Becky into Weslake.' He turned towards the girl. 'We need some things from the mercantile. Make a list.'

'S-sure, Eli,' she answered, dully.

He looked her up and down. 'An' wash your face or somethin', you look a wreck.' He turned to Clay. 'What're you waitin' for, kid? Get movin'.'

Fifteen minutes later, Clay was driving the buckboard out of the dusty ranch courtyard. Once beyond the limits of the ranch he picked up the old Indian trail that was the shortest, if not the most obvious route to Weslake. He was conscious of the nearness of the young woman beside him. He longed to reach out and put an arm around her shoulders but resisted the temptation.

They sat in silence for the first part of the ninety minute journey, then Clay voiced his thoughts in an unrehearsed burst. 'Becky, why don't we just keep goin', never go back?'

Becky turned to look at him, her eyes wide, her mouth open in astonishment. 'Chet! What you sayin'? You . . . you

37

want to *leave* Eli an' . . . an'. . . ?' Her voice tailed off.

He stared straight ahead. 'Ain't you figured how I feel about you yet?' he said, unable to meet her eyes. 'I've got to get you away from . . . him. I can't stand how he treats you.'

She stared at him. 'Eli? I never realized. . . .'

'Yeah, well, now you know,' he said, still not looking at her.

She sighed. 'I can't leave him, Chet, you know that,' she said. 'If I did, Eli'd kill my pa. He's told me that more than once, an' he means it.'

'He knows your pa?' Clay turned to her in surprise. 'How come?'

'I ain't exactly sure,' Becky said. 'But when Eli heard I'd lived in Solace, an' that my pa owned the hotel there, it seemed to set him thinkin'. Anyways, ever since then he's threatened to kill Pa, if'n I should get any ideas about leavin' the ranch. So, you see, even if you took off, I couldn't go with you.'

'Then I'll just have to kill Eli first,' Clay said.

Even as he spoke the words, his gut told him otherwise. He would never be able to do it. To Clay, Eli was the personification of the devil, and just as terrifying.

She put a hand on his arm. 'He'll tire of me, Chet,' she said. 'Then he'll let me go.' She looked at him strangely. 'But I didn't know you felt that way about me.'

He avoided her eye. 'Yeah, well, I do,' he said. 'An' it's drivin' me crazy to watch him take you to his bed an' . . . an' to imagine what he does to you. Every time I watch him take you up those stairs, I want to kill him.'

She stifled a sob. 'I . . . I want to kill him sometimes,

too,' she said.

They drove the next mile in silence, along the dusty rutted trail that snaked through the valley. On one side was a curving line of hills, half covered with pines, their aromatic smell filling Clay's nostrils. Opposite, a wall of sandstone towered against the blue sky and scudding clouds.

Every so often, Becky glanced across at him, trying to fathom how she felt about him. Was he *in love* with her? Or did he just want to bed her, the way most men did? It had come as a shock to hear him express his feelings. But what did it matter? There was nothing either she or he could do about it. Not while Eli Pike was alive. Would the kid *really* kill Eli?

'You'd have to kill Silas, too,' she said at last. 'An' maybe Ray and Nate. They ain't likely to just stand by an' do nothin'.'

'I know,' he said.

'Don't even try it, Chet. Like I said, he'll get tired of me. Then, who knows, maybe we could go away together.' She put a hand on his arm and squeezed it gently. She knew he didn't really believe her, but it was nice to dream.

'How did you get hooked up with Eli an' the others, Chet?' she asked. 'I never knew the whole story.'

Clay shrugged. 'Nothin' secret about it.' He took a deep breath. 'I was on the run from the law after shootin' a barkeep in a town called Adam's Creek. Had to leave fast. Drifted a time, an' took whatever work I could get. Taught myself to use a gun an' cheat at cards. Then I managed to get into an argument with some *hombres* over a game of poker in Weslake. One of the other guys had a

39

sawn-off shotgun an' would've killed me, given half a chance. But Ray was across the room an' heard the argument. He butted in an' got me out of trouble.'

'Then got you into a whole heap more by "persuadin'" you to join up with Eli,' Becky guessed.

Clay nodded. 'Yeah.'

'Bet you've had second thoughts about hookin' up with him since then.'

Clay made no reply, and they spoke no more for the rest of the journey into Weslake. At some point, Becky put a hand through Clay's arm and snuggled closer.

Back at the Lazy O, the four men had finished dividing up the take from the hold-up and were sat around the room drinking.

Silas was questioning his brother. 'You sure you can trust Garrod, Eli? He looks as sly as a fox, an' we're countin' on him, ain't we?'

'He'll do what he's said he'll do,' Eli said.

'How can you be sure?' Silas said.

'We have a deal, for one thing, and he knows I won't take kindly to him double-crossin' us,' Eli said. ' 'Sides, he's mighty anxious to get Becky back, ain't he?'

'He's gonna get her back, is he, Eli?' Ray Riggins put in. 'I mean, you're gonna let her go, are you?'

A half smile twitched at the corners of Eli's mouth. 'Ain't decided yet, have I?' He turned towards Nate Morgan. 'You clear about what you gotta do tomorrow, Nate?'

Morgan looked up from his whittling and shrugged. 'Sure.'

'We need a good coupl'a hours,' Eli reminded him, 'so be sure to lead 'em far enough away afore you lose 'em.'

'How can you be sure they'll form a posse an' go after him?' Ray wanted to know. 'There's no guarantee.'

' 'Cause Garrod's been told to raise hell if'n there looks like bein' any question of it, that's how,' Eli said. 'An' he's got influence in Solace. Now quit worryin', Ray.'

'You plannin' on hurtin' Garrod any, Nate?' Silas asked. ''Cause that'd look more . . . what's the word?'

'Realistic,' Ray supplied.

'Yeah, realistic,' Silas said. 'Gotta look real, ain't it?'

Nate sniffed. 'It'll look real.'

CHAPTER FIVE

Seven hours' ride away from the Lazy O, the town of Solace lay hot and airless, a brassy sun fixed in a cloudless blue sky. Sheriff Floyd Wickes stood by the window of his office and peered up Main Street, stroking the grey stubble on his chin. Floyd only visited Parnell's barber shop for a shave twice a week, and he wasn't due to stop by for another two days. Gaunt of face and thin as a rake, Floyd favoured a quiet life. He wasn't married, and rarely sought the company of a professional lady, preferring the comforts of a bottle of red-eye of an evening.

'Not a thing happenin',' he said, a satisfied expression on his face. 'Not a damn soul to be seen.'

Tom Walsh, his twenty-two-year old deputy, was sitting in the sheriff's chair reading a dime novel, his feet perched on the desk in front of him. He was lean and wiry, with a shock of straw-coloured hair and honest brown eyes. His addiction to dime novels was something Floyd failed to understand but tolerated, as Tom was a reliable deputy and a good friend.

'I tell a lie.' Floyd corrected himself after a moment.

'Harvey Garrod's just headed out of the bank as I speak.'

Floyd watched the half-stooped figure of the owner of Solace's only hotel walk across the dust-covered street, clearly deep in thought and moving like a man with the troubles of the state on his shoulders.

'Prob'ly been to see Arthur Makin about tonight's council meetin',' Floyd said. 'Prob'ly been makin' some excuse not to go, if I know Harvey.'

'Maybe,' Tom said, finally abandoning his book and looking up.

'You noticed how *distracted* Harvey's been jus' lately?' Floyd said. 'Like he's got somethin' on his mind. Somethin' that might be keepin' him from his sleep most nights. An' whatever it is, it seems to be agein' him fast. Not a well-lookin' man, our Harvey. Reckon he should pay a visit to Doc McFee.'

Tom shrugged. 'Can't say I've noticed,' he admitted.

'Seems to be since his daughter went to live with relatives up north someplace,' Floyd said. 'An' that was some time ago.'

'Guess Harvey misses her, him bein' a widower,' Tom said.

'A headstrong kinda girl, Becky Garrod,' Floyd opined.

Tom laughed. 'She sure is. Chased about every young man in town afore she left. Me included. And for a while there . . . she and I . . . well never mind. Becky sure is the biggest flirt I ever knew.'

'Got too much for Harvey to handle,' Floyd agreed.

'Not a bit like my Meg,' Tom said.

Floyd turned away from the window and grinned at him. '*Your* Meg!' he said, chuckling. 'Well, I guess that answers my question about whether or not you two young-sters were plannin' on gettin' married sometime soon, don't it?'

Tom blushed. 'Well, it ain't really a secret. Half the town seems to know it. We're thinkin' about a spring weddin'.'

'You expectin' her to live in that tumbledown shack of yours?' Floyd wanted to know. 'She won't take kindly to that after she's been livin' all nice an' comfortable with her aunt an' uncle over the mercantile these past months.'

'Nope, as a matter of fact I ain't,' Tom said. 'Accordin' to Doc McFee, Lily Carver's place will be comin' vacant soon. He reckons she ain't got more'n six months afore she goes to meet her Maker. An' I'll be lookin' to buy her house for Meg an' me. I've had a quiet word with Mr Makin at the bank, an' he reckons he'll be able to help out with some kinda loan or mortgage.'

'That right?' Floyd said. 'So you've been savin' your money?'

Tom nodded. 'Yeah,' he said, quietly. 'Started soon after Meg came to live in Solace. Knew straightaway she was the girl I wanted to spend the rest of my life with.' He glanced up, suddenly embarrassed. 'Don't know why I'm tellin' you all this.'

'Didn't need to. Guessed most of it for myself,' Floyd said.

'You did?'

'Sure I did,' Floyd answered.

'Well, like I said, it ain't no secret,' Tom said. 'Like it ain't no secret she's the prettiest girl this town's likely to see.'

'Changin' the subject an' speakin' of money,' Floyd

said. 'Ain't the cash for the mine's wages due at the bank this week?'

'Arrived yesterday afternoon, when you were takin' your nap,' Tom told him. 'Ready to go to the Marston office on Friday.'

'Oh, that right?' Floyd looked suitably embarrassed at his oversight.

'It's OK, Floyd. I watched it go into the bank,' Tom reassured him. 'Not that there's ever been any trouble.'

'Always a first time,' Floyd said.

The Marston silver mine lay twelve miles outside of the town's limits. It wasn't the biggest of silver mines, but it was Solace's biggest employer of men, together with the fifty or so more who lived in a camp on the outskirts of the town and brought vital business to the local traders. And whilst Solace's two saloons and three cafés were usually quiet by day, at night and at weekends they came alive, and especially after the mine's monthly payday.

Floyd moved away from the window, the strong midday sun beginning to hurt his eyes. 'Think I'll get myself a beer over at the Crazy Dog. You gonna join me?'

'Nope,' Tom said. 'We're needin' more coffee. Think I'll go get some.'

'An' I don't need to guess where you'll be gettin' it,' Floyd said, a twinkle in his eye.

CHAPTER SIX

Chester Green's mercantile was on the opposite side of Main Street, situated between the barber's shop and the corn merchant's. It was a medium-sized store, and in the happy position of having no competition, being the only mercantile in Solace. Chester Green and his wife, Carrie, owned and ran the store, more recently with the help of their niece, Meg, since the latter had come to live with them a year previously, a happy arrangement that suited all three of them. That hot, sultry afternoon, Meg was behind the counter, her clothes sticking to her, checking supplies when Tom entered.

'Howdy, beautiful,' he said, grinning. The aromatic smell of tobacco, coffee, spices and herbs filled his nose.

She smiled at him. 'Let me guess. You need more coffee. Never did know a pair like you and Sheriff Wickes for running out of coffee. What do you do, take baths in the stuff?'

Tom looked sheepish. 'Truth is, we ain't run out. I jus' needed an excuse to come an' see my girl.'

He vaulted over the counter and took her in his arms.

'An' is she beautiful? Yep!'

'Shh!' she chided him. 'Uncle Chester's upstairs taking his nap.'

'An' your aunt?'

'Aunt Carrie's at the church hall, helping to get things ready for tonight's church social.'

A lascivious grin spread across Tom's face and he tightened his grip. 'Then I think I'll jus' lock the door an' . . .'

'Tom Walsh, you'll do no such thing!' Meg said, pretending to be shocked and easing herself from his grasp.

'Aw, now, don't pretend you don't like it when I squeeze you some,' he chided.

'Well, now you come to mention it, I reckon I do,' she admitted, avoiding his eye. 'But if you've got some time on your hands you can help me check these supplies we had delivered yesterday. Otherwise I'll see you at the church social.'

'Jus' you be sure to keep every dance for me. No waltzin' off with some other young buck.'

Meg tossed her head, playfully. 'Well, I'll just have to see, won't I?' she said. She made a face. 'At least Becky Garrod isn't here any more to chase after every boy in town, including you! Reckon those relatives she's gone to stay with will have their hands full keeping her out of trouble.'

'Floyd an' me were talkin' about that earlier,' Tom said. 'We were sayin' Mr Garrod looks as though he is missin' her. Or that maybe somethin' else was troublin' him. We reckon he looks ill.'

Meg nodded. 'Uncle Chester was saying the same thing.' She gave him a kiss on the cheek. 'Anyway, I can't stand here gossiping, I've things to do, seeing as you clearly aren't going to help me check these supplies.'

Tom sighed. 'Guess I'll have to be goin' then.' He kissed her firmly on the mouth, leaving her almost breathless, then vaulted back over the counter.

'You don't want any coffee to take back then?' she said.

'Coffee? Who said anythin' about coffee? Pick you up at six.' He winked as he went out of the door.

A glow of pleasure spread through Meg's body as she watched him stride across the street, arms swinging jauntily at his sides and a spring in his step. A year ago when she first came to live with her aunt and uncle, it would have seemed inconceivable that she could ever feel such happiness, such contentment.

After Clay's desperate leave-taking, followed by her father dying suddenly from a heart attack, after defying the doctor's earlier predictions that he wouldn't last more than a few months after Clay went on the run, Meg had been at the lowest point of her life. The prospect of living alone and trying to scrape a living from the land had daunted her beyond description. And anyway, the place seemed to be haunted with her father's presence, which only intensified the pain she was feeling each day.

So when the letter from Solace arrived, reminding her that she had an alternative, she had been only too willing take up Uncle Chester's offer to go and start a new life with him and her Aunt Carrie, living and working at the mercantile. Indeed, it had seemed – and had since proved to be – an answer to her prayers.

After the decision had been made, things had moved quickly. Within a few days, the Adam's Creek bank had taken the homestead in payment for Matthew Thornton's outstanding mortgage, Meg had sold their few sticks of furniture to friends and neighbours, and she was boarding the first stage out of the town, ready with excited anticipation for the two-day journey north to Solace.

Not everything was picture perfect. Sometimes, when she couldn't sleep or when she had time on her hands, she thought about her brother, Clay. She wondered where he was, what he was doing, whether or not he missed her. They had been close right up until the time he'd gone on the run.

But for the most part she immersed herself in the everyday business of helping her aunt and uncle to run the store, enjoying the social life of a small western town, and dreaming of a life married to the man she loved.

Just one small shadow came between her and complete happiness with Tom. She hadn't told him about Clay. As far as Tom knew, she was an only child, a fiction she had persuaded her aunt and uncle to go along with, against their better judgement.

'Are you sure about this, Meg?' her aunt had said. 'Tom's an understanding young man. He's not the sort to hold a wayward brother against you.'

'Maybe I'll tell him at some point,' she had replied. 'Not just yet. Let me pick the right moment.'

It was a moment that had yet to arrive.

CHAPTER SEVEN

At eleven-fifteen the next morning Harvey Garrod sat in a swivel chair behind a large walnut desk in his office downstairs in the Solace Palace hotel in Solace's Main Street. He was trying to steady his nerves. He poured himself a third glass of whiskey from the bottle on his desk, his hand shaking. The chair he was sitting in creaked under his weight as, restlessly, he swung it to and fro, unable to concentrate on the accounts book in front of him. None of the columns seemed to add up right. Each time he totted them up, the figures seemed to blur in front of his eyes.

For the umpteenth time he took the silver timepiece from his vest pocket and checked it. Sometime between ten and eleven had been the arrangement, so where was Eli Pike's man?

'He'll be here,' he told himself. 'He has to be here!' Yet at the same time, part of him hoped the man wouldn't show up; that he wouldn't have to go through with the plan.

But where would that leave Becky? In the hands of the Pike Gang!

He had learned of Becky's fate ten days after the stage-coach hold-up. The aunt to whom his daughter had been sent had wired Harvey when Becky hadn't arrived.

Then he'd had the message from Eli Pike.

It had come in the form of a scribbled note, shoved under his outside office door late one night four weeks after the kidnap. He had discovered it the following morning.

IF YOU WANT YOUR DAUGHTER BACK, BE AT CROCKER'S PASS 6AM WEDNESDAY. MAYBE WE CAN DO A DEAL. TELL NOBODY, OR SHE'S DEAD MEAT.

A horrified Harvey had complied – and learned the identity of the gang leader who was holding Becky. *Eli Pike!* It was Harvey's worst nightmare come true.

Pike, together with two of his cohorts as back-up, had arrived at Crocker's Pass fifteen minutes after Harvey. A deal had been struck. A deal that would make a criminal out of Harvey but might – just might – save his daughter. Always assuming Eli Pike could be trusted.

And even Harvey had to admit that that was a bold assumption.

Now everything was ready. Earlier Harvey had unlocked the door at the rear of the hotel, leading into the passage outside his office. Later he would 'confess' to having forgotten to lock it the night before, should anyone question it. And he was sure the sheriff *would* question it. Floyd

Wickes was no fool, and neither was that deputy of his. He would have to be convincing.

Harvey's office was well away from the lobby of the hotel, so there was no danger of the desk clerk hearing anything. It would be just bad luck if the clerk decided to pay him a visit to make some query during the next half hour or so. Harvey glanced back at the safe in the wall behind him. Earlier, he had removed most of the cash – $250 – and secured it in one of his desk drawers. It wasn't important to the plan that Pike's man got away with any money, only that he appeared to have done so, he told himself.

It was then that he heard the familiar creak of the passage floorboards and knew that the time had come.

He swallowed the rest of the glass of whiskey – and waited.

'Just stay calm,' he muttered to himself. 'Think of Becky.'

Seconds later, Garrod's office door eased open and Nate Morgan stood, unsmiling, in the doorway. He wore his usual long brown riding duster, and after glancing around, pushed back the rim of his hat and stepped into the room. He moved unhurriedly across to the desk.

Harvey stared at him, his mouth dry 'You're . . . you're late.'

Nate ignored this and nodded towards the safe.

'Open it.'

Harvey took a key from one of his desk drawers and heaved his corpulent form out of his chair. With his hands still shaking he managed to unlock the safe. Inside were a few dollar bills and a sheaf of documents tied with a ribbon, nothing else. He turned to face the other man.

Nate smiled a crooked smile. 'What's the matter, Garrod? Don't you trust me?'

'It only has to *look* like you robbed me, that was the arrangement,' Harvey said, trying to maintain a modicum of dignity but aware from the feeling in his gut that he was suddenly in urgent need of a privy. 'Did . . . did you bring some rope to tie me?' he asked, sitting back in his chair again.

Nate shook his head. 'Won't need it,' he said.

And with that he removed his six-gun from its holster, and taking hold of it by the barrel, slugged Harvey across the head.

Harvey collapsed unconscious, corkscrewing on to the floor in a heap.

Nate stared at him for a moment, then smiled to himself.

'Not 'xactly what you expected, was it, Garrod?' he muttered, grinning.

He decided to use the hotel owner's own belt to tie his hands behind his back. Next he moved to the desk and began systematically opening drawers and tossing them and their contents on to the floor until he found the wad of cash Harvey had taken from the safe earlier.

'Nice try, Garrod,' he muttered. 'Reckon I'm due a bonus.'

Grinning to himself, he stuffed the banknotes into his shirt, snatched up the bottle of whiskey from the desk, glanced around for a final time, then left, leaving the office door open behind him.

He walked swiftly to where his piebald gelding was

waiting at the back of the hotel, mounted up and headed out of town.

Minutes later, a groggy Harvey Garrod came to, his head throbbing like a jack hammer. He groaned and looked up at the ransacked desk, then saw the drawers scattered around him on the floor, including the drawer where the money had been.

Empty.

Harvey swore. He looked for the bottle of whiskey and found that it, too, had vanished. Not that he could have reached it with his hands tied behind his back.

'*Bastard*!' he said, before passing out again.

Nate Morgan made a wide but clearly visible trail as he left Solace, heading towards the hills and travelling the best part of fifteen miles before turning off amongst a thick stand of pine trees, the fallen needles softening the sound of his horse's hoofs.

He rode at a steady pace, calmly and with little thought beyond the trail his mount was laying for others to follow. It was exactly what Eli had told him to do.

After taking several swigs of whiskey, he made sure he left signs of his passing before entering a narrow canyon with huge overhanging boulders. A mile further on, he turned off again. After this, he made certain his tracks were erased before taking his horse along a dry, stony riverbed, then seeking out a trail that led to a derelict trapper's shack.

Once there, and comforting himself with the stolen bottle of whiskey, he spent the next couple of hours counting the money he'd stolen from Harvey Garrod, well satisfied with his morning's work. Now it was up to Eli and the others to make the most of his diversion. Nate had no doubts that they would.

CHAPTER EIGHT

It was shortly after midday before Louie Smart, the hotel desk clerk, got to wondering why he hadn't seen Harvey that morning. Usually the manager came to see him with a list of instructions for the day. Worried, Louie decided to pay a visit to Harvey's office.

He entered the room just as the hotel owner, still on the floor with his hands strapped behind his back, seemed to be coming to.

'Jeeze, Mr Garrod,' the clerk said, hurrying to undo Harvey's belt and free his hands. 'What happened?' Then he saw the open, empty safe. 'Jeeze!' he said again.

A still semi-dazed Harvey heaved himself up into a sitting position with difficulty, touched the side of his head and stared at the blood on his fingers. Then he threw up over the floor.

'Guess I'll get Doc McFee,' Louie said, edging towards the door.

'And the sheriff,' Harvey said, weakly.

After the clerk had gone, he tried to collect his thoughts. What the hell had happened? There had been nothing in the plan about hitting him over the head. He stared again at the empty safe, then at the scattered empty drawers, including the one in which he'd put the money. Nor about stealing any money. It was only supposed to *appear* as if a robbery had taken place. Harvey was supposed to back up the fiction that he'd had several hundred dollars in the safe.

He swore to himself. 'That bastard Pike! I was a damn fool to trust him; to trust any of the Pike gang.'

Louie returned after a few minutes. 'Doc's on his way, Mr Garrod,' he said. 'Sheriff Wickes, too. You gonna be all right? Can I get you anything? You don't look too perky.'

'I don't feel too damn perky either,' Harvey groaned. He nodded to a cabinet by the door. 'Open it,' he told the clerk. 'There's a bottle of whiskey in there. Pour me a slug.'

The desk clerk did as he was asked and Harvey took the shot in one mouthful. He held out the glass.

'Again,' he said.

There was a repeat performance by the two men, then Louie helped Harvey into the chair behind his desk where he sat holding his head in his hands. Moments later, Doc McFee, Tom Walsh and the sheriff arrived together.

'Hell, Harvey, who did this to you?' Floyd wanted to know.

Doc McFee held up a hand. 'Hold on a minute, Floyd. Let me take a look at him.' He examined the wound on Harvey's head. 'Nasty,' he said. 'You're going to have a bump the size of an egg.'

'Hurts like hell,' Harvey agreed.

'You could be suffering from concussion, Harvey,' the

doc said. 'Best take it easy for an hour or two, maybe longer.'

'I'll be fine, doc,' Harvey answered.

'Tell us what happened,' Tom said.

'Look around you! A robbery, that's what happened,' Harvey said. 'Emptied the damn safe.'

'Go on,' Floyd said.

By the time Doc McFee had patched him up, Harvey had told his story about an unknown raider robbing his safe and knocking him out. He said nothing about the money missing from the desk drawer.

'How did he get in?' Tom asked.

'Reckon I forgot to lock the rear door,' Harvey said.

'Any idea who he was?' Floyd asked.

'No. Like I said, he was masked.'

'What was he built like?' Tom asked. 'I mean, was he tall? Short? Fat? Thin? What was he wearin', apart from the mask?'

'How in hell do I know!' Harvey growled. 'The bastard hit me over the head almost as soon as he came through the door!'

'When did it happen, Harvey?' Doc McFee asked.

'About eleven this morning, I think,' Harvey told him. 'I'm not sure.' He looked at the sheriff. 'What are you going to do?'

Floyd looked at the clock fixed to the wall of Harvey's office. 'He's had a good two hours' head start,' he said.

'You're going after him, aren't you?' Harvey said. 'You aren't just going to let him get away?'

'No, I guess not.' Floyd looked at his deputy. 'Tom, rustle up a handful of men to form a posse and we'll go after him. Maybe we'll get lucky.'

Tom hurried away. Floyd waited until he had gone, then turned back to Harvey. He frowned. There was something about the hotel owner's story that didn't ring true to Floyd's ears.

'So how did the raider know you'd accidentally forgotten to lock the rear door of the hotel?' he asked the hotel owner. 'You made it kinda easy for him to get in without the desk clerk or anyone else at the hotel being aware of it. Pretty damn convenient, don't you reckon, Harvey?'

'Eh? What're you suggesting?' Harvey retorted, pouring himself another slug of whiskey. He was still groggy from the blow Nate had given him, but thinking clearly enough to register Floyd's suspicious tone.

'I ain't suggestin' anythin',' Floyd said. 'Just askin'.'

'Well, I don't have an answer,' Harvey said, hotly, avoiding the sheriff's eye. He glanced at Doc McFee. 'I don't feel so good, doc. Maybe you're right, maybe I am suffering from concussion.'

Doc McFee turned to the sheriff. 'Best to take it easy on him for now, Floyd. Maybe come and talk to him again later.'

Floyd nodded reluctantly. 'Whatever you say, Doc. Guess I'll go an' see if'n Tom's got that posse together.'

Half an hour later, Floyd, Tom and a posse of fifteen townsmen rode out of Solace, more in hope than expectation. Floyd and Tom rode side by side, the two men in conversation.

'Did you feel there was somethin' – I don't know – *odd* about Harvey's explanation?' Floyd said.

'Like what?' Tom said.

'Can't put my finger on it, but there was somethin' too pat about it all – the door bein' left unlocked when there was money in the safe, an' the raider knowin' about it?'

'What're you sayin', Floyd?'

'I don't know what I'm sayin',' Floyd admitted.

'Well, let's just catch the critter an' then we'll know,' Tom said.

'Critter's had best part of three hours' start on us, Tom,' Floyd said. 'I ain't hopeful.'

CHAPTER NINE

Just after three o'clock, Eli and his three accomplices rode into Solace. They hitched their horses to the rail outside the bank. Then, moving casually but taking in the near-empty street and the overall quietness of the town, they removed the empty saddle-bags from their horses and entered through the front door of the building.

An elderly woman passed them in the doorway as she made her way out into the street. Eli turned his face away quickly. She looked surprised but walked on without looking back. Later, she would be vague about giving a description to the sheriff, other than to say the man was mean-looking with a beard, and that she'd paid no attention to the others.

Silas and Ray followed Eli into the bank, and Clay brought up the rear. Each man pulled up his neckerchief to mask the lower half of his face as he entered.

There were no other customers, just a single bank teller behind the counter and the manager in his glass-partitioned office at the back. The manager's name was painted on the glass panel in the door – Mr Arthur Makin.

The teller looked up and saw the group of masked men. His eyes widened, his jaw dropped, and a small startled cry came from somewhere at the back of his throat.

'Oh, hell. . . !' he began.

'Take it easy, mister,' Eli told him, unholstering his six-gun. 'Do somethin' stupid and you'll have a bullet through your head.'

'OK, OK!' The white-faced teller put his hands in the air and stepped back.

Clay closed both doors of the bank and leaned against them. He handed Eli his saddle-bag, then took out his .45 and held it loosely by his side. He could hear his heart thumping in his chest. He had never taken part in a bank raid. In the past, he'd only had the job of minding the horses whilst the others went into the bank. But today Eli had insisted that he take a full part in the raid. It seemed to be another 'test' of Clay's mettle.

Eli and Ray went through the counter flap to the manager's office as Silas leaned on the counter and pointed his six-gun at the teller.

'Jus' do like we tell you an' nobody'll get hurt,' Silas told him. He put his saddle-bag on the counter. 'Now fill that with cash. Pronto.'

The manager, seeing what was happening, had risen from his desk. He started to remove something from his desk drawer but Ray reached across and shoved his .45 into the manager's stomach.

'I wouldn't do that, if I were you,' he said, slamming the drawer shut on the other man's hand and cuffing him across the face with his gloved fist.

62

The manager gasped with pain and fell back into his chair.

'Now,' Eli said, 'this is what's gonna happen. You're gonna take me an' my friend up to the room out back where the safe is, an' you're gonna put all the cash into these saddle-bags. An' any left over, you're gonna shove into canvas moneybags. Got that?'

Arthur Makin nodded, nursing his injured hand. 'Yes, sir,' he said. 'Yes, indeed. Whatever you say.' He wore black trousers, a chalk-striped jacket over a grey vest and a spotted tie. A damp patch appeared at his crotch as he eased himself from his chair.

'Let's go,' Eli said.

Across the street from the bank, Chester Green watched and smiled as his niece left the mercantile. It was a smile of contentment. A smile of satisfaction. It had been a real pleasure having Meg living with them this past year. And it had been nice company for Carrie, having another female around the place.

Chester and his wife had no children of their own, and Carrie had 'adopted' Meg as a daughter almost as soon the girl had arrived.

'Meg gone to the bank?' Carrie asked now, coming from the back room of the store.

'Yes,' Chester answered. 'She won't be long, now there's no chance of her meeting with Tom for a chat. He's gone with the posse.'

Carrie shook her head. 'What a terrible thing to have happened at the Palace. Poor Mr Garrod, I hope he's recovering.'

63

Word about the robbery at the hotel had spread rapidly once a posse had been formed.

Chester nodded. 'Doc McPhee said Harvey took a nasty hit over the head.'

Carrie turned towards the back room. 'I'll make some fresh coffee for when Meg returns,' she said.

Chester smiled. 'She'll appreciate that.'

Meg Thornton made her way across the street from the mercantile. She wore a wide-brimmed straw hat to protect her face from the searing mid-afternoon sun. Her underclothes stuck to her body and her cotton dress was limp from the heat. In one hand she carried a reticule containing the last three days' takings from the mercantile.

Still shocked by what she had heard had happened at the Solace Palace hotel earlier, and worried about Tom who was out somewhere chasing the raider, she barely noticed that the bank doors were closed until she had almost reached them. Surprised and a little curious, she pushed against them, only to feel a resistance from the other side.

'That's odd,' she murmured.

She frowned and knocked loudly. It was too early for the bank to be closed, so what was happening? She was certain neither Howie Clark or Mr Makin had gone with the posse, but maybe one of them had been taken ill.

Her hand was raised to knock again when she noticed the four horses tethered at the hitching rail. Before she could reflect on the significance of this, the bank door opened suddenly, a hand gripped her arm and she was yanked inside, the door slamming shut again behind her.

A .45 was pressed against her head.

'Wh . . . what. . . ?' she began.

'Jus' relax an' don't do anything' to. . . .' The words trailed off and there was a sharp intake of breath, followed by, '*M-Meg?*'

Meg whirled round and stared at the masked speaker. She gasped when she saw the knife scar over his left eye and heard the once-familiar voice.

'*Clay!*'

He released her and she stepped away from him, trying to take in what was happening.

'Clay, what. . . ?' she began.

Another masked man, with thick black hair and a lazy eye above the mask, was pointing a gun at a shaking Howie Clark, the teller, as Howie stuffed banknotes into a saddle-bag. The latter looked equally surprised that Meg seemed to recognize one of the raiders.

They're robbing the bank.

The thought struck Meg like a physical blow, and she reeled under its impact.

'Well, well, ain't this a surprise!' The raider at the counter was chuckling beneath his mask. He waved his six-gun between Meg and her brother. 'You two know each other?'

Meg glanced at Clay but said nothing. She was visibly shaking and her mouth was suddenly dry as the desert. She looked towards the manager's office and saw it was empty. Where was Mr Makin?

'She . . . she's my sister,' Clay said. 'Meg, what're you doin'. . . ?'

'Well, ain't that nice.' The other man laughed. 'Wait a

minute. She called you *Clay*. You been hidin' behind a false name, Chet?' He moved away from the counter and stepped towards Meg. He put an arm round her shoulder. 'Anyways, ain't this cosy? Howdy, Sis!'

Meg flinched and tried to move away, but his grip was firm. '*Please!*' she said.

'Leave her, Silas!' Clay said.

The man with the lazy eye ignored him. 'Kinda pretty, too,' he said. 'Too pretty to be a *sister.*'

'Silas, I'm warning you!' Clay said.

Silas paid no attention to the threat as, smiling, his hand slid from Meg's shoulder and down under the bodice of her dress and chemise until it was cupping her breast.

She let out a gasp.

'Quit it, Silas!' Clay yelled. 'Leave her alone!'

Silas gave a snort of derision. 'Aw, come on kid. I ain't gonna hurt her. Jus' havin' a bit of harmless fun, ain't I?'

Clay levelled his gun so that it was pointing at Silas. 'Get away from her!'

Still chuckling, Silas stared at Clay for several seconds then said, 'Maybe I'll take her with me when we finish up here. She'd be company for Becky. Now, let's jus' see . . .' And with one swift movement, he ripped open the front of Meg's dress and chemise, laughing loudly. 'Pretty, eh?'

Whimpering and clutching her torn clothes, Meg somehow managed to pull away from him.

Silas reached for her again . . .

. . . *and Clay shot him.*

The bullet took Silas in the neck. His knees sagged, and with a choking sound and an astonished look in his eyes, he dropped to the floor. Blood seeped around the corners of his neckerchief mask, which slipped from his face as he clutched at it. There was a final gurgling noise, and then he was silent.

Out of the corner of his eye, Clay saw Howie Clark reach for and lift the six-shooter that had been concealed under the counter. Before Howie could take aim with his trembling hand, Clay whirled and shot him.

Meg let out a little scream.

Howie slumped to the floor, dragging the saddle-bag of money with him and scattering notes and coins around him.

'*Silas? Chet? What'n hell's goin' on down there? You OK?*'

The shout came from the upstairs back room, followed by the sound of feet coming swiftly down the stairs.

A terrified Meg looked at Clay. 'Who. . . ?' she began.

He put a finger to his lips to stop her, yanked the door open. '*Run!*' he said.

CHAPTER TEN

Floyd, Tom and the posse reached the narrow box canyon where the trail suddenly seemed to peter out. The rutted ground was baked hard as flint. Each man following drew his horse to a halt in a cloud of white trail dust and looked towards Floyd for further instructions.

Floyd took off his hat and wiped sweat from his forehead with his neckerchief. 'Looks like our man decided to cover his tracks from here on,' he said to Pete Deakin, Solace's liveryman and the member of the posse who pulled up alongside of him. 'Trail's run out.'

Pete nodded his agreement. 'Gonna take hours to pick it up again.'

Tom sat astride his horse a yard or two behind them, looking thoughtful. The air was thin and hot and he had the taste of dust in his mouth. He pushed back his Stetson and began to build a smoke. Something was bothering him.

'But why leave it until now?' he pondered. 'The critter leaves a trail that's so clear a kid could follow it. Then, suddenly, he decides to cover his tracks.'

'Yeah, it's strange,' Floyd agreed.

'Almost as though he's been leadin' us a dance up to now,' Pete said.

The other men in the posse seemed to be waiting for Floyd to make a decision. They moved their horses to form a circle around him.

'I've been thinkin' this past mile or two. Guess he'd know we'd get a posse together to run him down,' Tom said. 'Wouldn't 'xactly be a surprise.' He drew on his smoke and rubbed a hand against the side of his face.

'So?' Pete said. 'What's on your mind, Tom?'

'Suppose . . . he *wanted* us to follow him.'

'*Wanted us to?*' Floyd said. 'Don't make sense. What sort of owlhoot *wants* to be chased by a posse?'

'One who wants us to follow him this far, until we were best part of two hours from Solace, before losin' us,' Tom said.

'But why?' Pete said.

'Yeah, what're you sayin'?' Floyd said.

'Those tracks of his were too obvious,' Tom said, looking up at the rocky side of the canyon. He drew on his cigarette and exhaled a cloud of smoke. 'No, the critter wanted us out of town for some reason.'

'What reason?' Pete persisted.

They were silent for several moments, pondering. Then Pete Floyd said, 'You mean he's been a . . . a kind'a *decoy*?'

'Guess I do,' Tom said.

Ty Brooks, another member of the posse who had been listening in on the conversation, said, 'Jus' supposin' you're right, then why was he so all-fired anxious to get us away from the town? What's gonna happen in Solace today?'

. 'That's the big question,' Tom said.

They sat in contemplative silence for several minutes, looking at the empty trail ahead and considering the next step.

'Jeeze!' Tom said suddenly. 'The bank!'

'What about the bank?' Ty said.

Tom tossed his cigarette to the ground. '*The payroll! The mine's payroll!*'

Realization swept over Floyd as his face paled. 'A bank raid, that's what's goin' to happen.' He dry-swallowed. 'We're goin' back!'

And he turned his horse around.

The others followed suit.

CHAPTER ELEVEN

Eli burst out of back stairs, gun at the ready. He took in the scene in an instant. Two dead bodies – his brother's and the bank teller's – and a white-faced Clay.

'Jesus! What happened, Chet?'

'The . . . the teller . . . he had . . . a gun under the counter,' Clay stammered.

'He shot Silas?' Eli said.

'Y-yeah, Eli,' Clay said, nodding violently. 'Yeah, that's right. An' . . . an' I shot him.'

Ray, with two bulging saddle-bags slung over his shoulder, appeared with the bank manager from the back stairs. Both men took in the scene, the manager letting out a small cry.

Eli turned to them. 'The teller had a gun an'. . . .' he began.

'Yeah, I heard,' Ray said. He turned and stared hard at Clay, a sceptical look on his face. 'I thought I heard a scream, Chet. Sounded like a woman.'

'It . . . it was the teller,' Clay said.

'Is that right?' Ray said. He pushed the manager away

from him so that the little man stumbled and fell on to his hands and knees. 'We gotta get outa here, Eli. Those shots will have been heard outside.'

'Yeah, they will,' Eli said, eyes wild with a mixture of fury and despair as he turned to look down at the manager. 'So one more won't make a damn bit of difference, especially as I guess you've realized who we are!' He levelled his .45.

'No! Please, Mr Pike! I won't tell . . .' Arthur Makin pleaded – before Eli shot him in the chest. The manager fell back on to the floor.

'Let's go!' Eli said.

Clay, still stunned by all that had happened, seemed incapable of moving. He stared stupidly at the fallen man, bile rising in his throat.

'*Chet*!' Eli yelled. 'I said, let's go!'

Clay forced himself to move, wrenched open the bank door and looked out into the street. He saw the back of Meg as she neared the mercantile. She was half-running, looking back from time to time.

Clay ran towards his horse and unhitched it from the rail.

Inside the bank, Eli picked up his brother's body, heaved it over his shoulder and followed Clay into the street.

Ray started to follow him, then hesitated and dodged behind the counter. He pulled the saddle-bag, half full of cash, from Howie's deathly grasp. He scooped up a handful of the scattered notes and coins from the floor then, as an afterthought, leaned across and carefully removed the six-shooter from Howie's other hand. A

72

frown creased his forehead as his fingers went round the barrel.

'*Cold*,' he muttered, nodding to himself. '*Like I figured it would be.*' He shoved the gun into his belt and hurried after Eli and Clay.

Outside, Eli was manoeuvring Silas's body over the dead man's horse and tying it down. Clay was already sitting astride his own mount, gun in hand and looking up and down the street for any possible threat. Once or twice he thought he saw a face at a window or in a doorway, but nobody ventured outside, or if they did, they retreated swiftly. The only figure visible was Meg as she half ran on to the boardwalk outside the mercantile where Chester and Carrie Green would be waiting for her. Clay could vaguely remember his aunt and uncle, having visited them when he was small. He reflected on how shocked they would be to learn their nephew was part of the Pike gang, an ache of misery in his chest.

Eli finished tying Silas's body to the saddle.

Ray climbed up on to his own horse and sidled the animal across to Clay. 'I picked up the teller's six-shooter,' he said quietly. 'An' you know somethin'?'

'What?' Clay said.

'The gun was cold,' Ray said. 'It hadn't been fired.'

'So there must've been another gun,' Clay said, avoiding the other man's eye. 'Maybe he had one under. . . .'

'Quit talkin' an' start ridin'!' Eli yelled, climbing aboard his own horse and moving off.

'We'll talk about this later, Clay,' Ray said softly.

Meg stumbled towards the door of the mercantile. At one

point she glanced back to see one of the men lifting the dead man's body over the saddle of one of the horses. A third man came out of the bank and, minutes later, all three rode away, one of them leading the dead raider's horse. She saw Clay's stetson blow off his head, revealing his thick brown hair. He glanced back at her, desperation etched across his face, but didn't stop.

At last, several townsfolk came out from buildings along the street, in time to see the riders gallop past. But they quickly retreated for cover when two of the three men turned and began firing random shots in their direction.

A startled Chester and Carrie Green, together with an old-timer who had been buying tobacco, emerged from the mercantile. They took one look at Meg and hurriedly ushered her into the store. Meg clutched the torn bodice of her dress in an effort to preserve her modesty.

'Dear God, Meg, what happened?' Carrie asked her niece. 'Did those men. . . ?' She pointed at Meg's tattered dress.

'No!' Meg said quickly. 'I . . . I fell.'

'Fell?' Chester Green said.

'Against the . . . the hitching post outside the bank,' Meg improvised. 'There . . . there must have been a nail. I tore my dress, and . . . I was on my way back here when shots came from the bank and . . . those men . . . well, you saw. . . .'

'Yes!' Chester said. 'And it looks like they robbed the bank!'

'Sure does!' said the old-timer. 'Who do you reckon they were?' He seemed unable to tear his eyes away from Meg's bosom.

Carrie Green scowled at him. 'Come through to the back room, Meg. You need to get out of that dress.' She guided her niece through the store. 'Mercy, I hope and pray Howie and Mr Makin are all right.'

'Me too,' said Chester. 'But those shots . . .'

Meg said nothing, her thoughts reeling at the shock of seeing her brother.

How in God's name had he become mixed up with a gang of bank raiders? What had he been doing these past years to get himself entangled with a bunch of desperados? Close to tears, for once she was glad her pa wasn't alive. He would have been deeply ashamed to learn of Clay's predicament.

Then another thought struck her. What would Tom think if he ever discovered it was her *brother* who had killed Howie Clark, the bank teller? Would that be the end of her and Tom? Would he – a lawman – want the sister of a killer for a wife?

Doc McFee watched the raiders disappear into the distance before grabbing his bag and running across to the bank. As did Chester Green and Saul Archer, the corn merchant – the only men, other than Frank Parker, the town undertaker, and Harvey Garrod and his clerk, who had not joined the sheriff's posse, all of them reckoned to be too old to go chasing after bandits.

Chester picked up the abandoned stetson from the middle of the street, glanced at it, but could see no distinguishing marks that would help identify its owner. He followed the others into the bank with a mounting dread.

They found Arthur Makin prostrate on the floor,

clutching his chest, blood seeping through his waistcoat and his fingers. His eyes were glassy and his breathing came in jerky spasms. The doc knelt down beside him whilst Chester went to find Howie. Saul Archer hovered in the doorway, shocked but unsure what to do.

'Take it easy, Arthur,' the doc said, pulling open his bag and taking in the extent of the bank manager's injury at the same time. He didn't like what his eyes were telling him. 'You're going to be all right.' He made a silent apology to his Maker for the deception: unless he was mistaken, Arthur had only minutes to live. He could also see the bank manager was trying to tell him something.

The doc put his ear to Arthur's mouth. 'What's that, my friend?'

'*P-Pike.*' Makin choked on the word.

'What did he say?' Saul asked.

'Sounded like "pipe",' Doc McFee said.

'Didn't know he smoked one,' Saul said.

Doc McFee leaned closer to the bank manager. 'You want your pipe, Arthur?'

But there was no answer to his question. There never would be, he realized. Arthur Makin had breathed his last breath.

Chester joined the doc. 'Gone?' he enquired, nodding at the bank manager.

'Yes,' the doc replied.

'Howie Clark's dead, too.'

'*What?*'

'Behind the counter.' Chester turned to Saul. 'Best go an' fetch Frank,' he said, meaning Frank Parker.

Saul nodded and hurried off.

'This is terrible,' the doc said. 'Who were those animals?'

'All four were too far ahead for me to recognize any faces as they rode away,' Chester told the doc. 'But one of them was dead. I could see his corpse slung over his horse.'

'I saw that,' the doc said. 'It accounts for one of the shots I heard. D'you think Howie or Arthur killed him?'

They were suddenly aware of Harvey Garrod listening to them in the bank doorway. How long he'd been there they couldn't have said.

'Harvey?' Doc McFee said. 'You OK now? You still look pretty sick to me.'

Harvey had crossed over from the Palace Hotel with Louie his desk clerk. Both of them were staring unbelievingly at Arthur Makin's prostrate form.

'Is he. . . ?' Louie asked.

The doc nodded. 'Dead, yeah,' he said. 'Howie Clark, too.'

'Sweet Jesus!' Harvey said, 'Did . . . did Arthur say anything before. . . ?'

'Nothing that made sense,' the doc said. 'Something about his pipe. Although I've never seen him with a pipe. Guess he was rambling.'

'P. . .pipe?' Harvey put a hand against the bank counter to steady himself, his face ashen.

Doc McFee looked concerned. 'Louie, take him back to the hotel. Take yourself off to bed, Harvey. By the looks of you, you haven't fully recovered from that knock on the head.'

'I . . . I guess I will,' Harvey said.

*

Meg was sitting in the back room of the mercantile. Her aunt, seeing how pale she looked, had insisted on giving her a drink of brandy before allowing her to go and change. Meg nursed the glass, twisting it between her fingers.

'Are you sure you're all right, dear?' Carrie said, her voice filled with concern. 'You've had a shock. If you hadn't torn your dress. . . .'

Meg tried to smile. 'I'll be fine, aunt.'

'Well, you were very lucky. Heaven knows what might have happened if you'd actually gone *into* the bank.'

Meg sipped the brandy and said nothing.

'Did you see *anything* of what was happening?' her aunt asked.

Meg shook her head. 'The bank door was shut. Which . . . which I thought was odd,' she added quickly. 'But then I tore my dress, so didn't think any more about it.'

What a cool liar I am, she thought. But how can I tell her what really happened? How can I tell her about Clay?

CHAPTER TWELVE

The doc watched Louie and Harvey leave. He looked thoughtful. 'Tell me something, Chester,' he said after a moment. 'How long is it since we had any kind of robbery in Solace?'

'Before today you mean?' Chester scratched his nose. 'Four, five years, at least,' he said. 'Probably longer. Why are you asking?'

'And now we get two *in one day*.' Doc McFee shook his head. 'First, Harvey gets his hotel safe robbed, then the bank's raided a few hours later.'

'What about it?' Chester said.

'Doesn't it strike you as strange? A bit too much of a coincidence?'

Chester stared at him. 'You sayin' they're connected?'

'Well, think about it,' the doc said. 'What happens after the hotel robbery? The sheriff and Tom Walsh get a posse together and chase after the robber, leaving just you, me, Saul and a few old-timers in town. Plus Arthur and Howie at the bank. A few hours later, by which time Floyd, Tom and the posse are miles away, the bank is raided.'

Chester frowned. 'So?'

'So there's no chance of gettin' *another* posse together, is there?' said the doc. 'So the bank raiders get away clean.'

'That's true,' Chester conceded. 'I wonder if Floyd and the others caught up with him – the man who robbed the hotel.'

'My guess is "no",' the doc said. 'He had too much of a head start, and he'll cover his tracks once the posse is well away from Solace. If my thinking is correct, the man was a decoy, intended to lure away most of the town's menfolk and the town's law.' He rubbed his chin, looking puzzled and casting an eye around the bank. 'But I still don't understand what exactly happened in here. Who could've killed the fourth bank raider?'

'Maybe Arthur or Howie had a gun concealed some-where and the raiders took it with them before they went off,' Chester suggested.

'Maybe. But I reckon something went wrong. Otherwise, why was it necessary to shoot Arthur and Howie? Neither was the kind to put up a fight. Why not just tie them up? Besides, there's still money here, cash they left behind, as if they left in a hurry, before they'd intended. No, there's something we're missing here, Chester.'

'Supposing you're right,' Chester said. 'Thing is, with both the witnesses dead, how are we going to find out what that something is?'

Moments later, Saul arrived back with Frank Parker, the

undertaker. The latter had clearly been told what to expect, and looked calmly at the dead Arthur Makin.

'There's two of them, Frank,' Chester said. 'Howie's behind the counter.'

Parker nodded.

'Guess we'll leave you to it then,' Doc McFee said.

Meg was sitting in her room at the back of the mercantile where her aunt had left her to change her torn clothes. She wasn't at all sure her aunt had been convinced by her story of a hitching post and a nail, judging by the way Carrie Green had eyed the rents in both Meg's dress and chemise, a quizzical expression on her face. But when Meg had offered no further explanation, she had been forced to accept the story. At least for now.

Meg's greater worry was the discovery of her brother's association with a gang of bandits. The name 'Silas' that she'd heard Clay call the other man in the bank, which she had immediately linked to the name 'Pike', were names she had heard Tom mention in relation to his work as a deputy. The Pike gang were notorious, suspected of some of the vilest crimes in the territory. But according to Tom, because of no hard proof, due mostly to dead or intimidated witnesses and a compliant sheriff in Weslake, the town where the Pike gang hung out, their criminal acts had always gone unpunished.

But now she was a witness, one who could testify that the Pike gang had in fact been the bank raiders. Except that, by doing so, she would implicate her own brother in the killings that had taken place. Indeed, had *carried out two of them.*

81

No, she would have to stick to her story. Even Tom mustn't know the truth. *Especially* Tom. But what about the third shot, the one that she'd heard after she had left the bank and was crossing the street? Logically, there was only one other possible victim, and that was Mr Makin, the manager.

The Pike gang rarely leave witnesses if they're recognized.

She'd heard Tom say this in the past. Now she knew it for a fact. But only Clay knew that Meg had been an eye-witness to Howie's and Silas Pike's murders, and he would say nothing to the other two men she had seen riding away with him, she could be certain of that.

But there had been another familiar name mentioned during the fracas – one spoken by Silas Pike. It hadn't really registered with Meg at the time, she had been too fearful about what was going to happen to her. But now, sitting in the quietness of her room, she remembered it clearly.

Becky.

Meg only knew one girl called Becky, and that was Becky Garrod – who had apparently gone to stay with rel-atives up north, but whose stay was turning out to be longer than most folk in town had been led to believe it would be. Becky, the girl who had a reputation for wild and impetuous behaviour. Behaviour that had been the bane of her father's life. Could it be a coincidence? Something told Meg it couldn't.

The question was, did Harvey Garrod know that his daughter might be involved with the Pike gang? Surely not, or he would have done something about it. One thing was clear, Meg thought: she couldn't tell him, not without revealing the fact that she'd been in the bank at the time of the robbery.

Oh, Clay! What have you got me mixed up in?

CHAPTER THIRTEEN

Floyd, Tom and a dispirited posse rode back into Solace early that evening. Before they had a chance to report on their lack of success, Doc McFee relayed the catastrophic events of the afternoon, and his suspicions about the robbery at the Palace hotel. They were sitting in the lobby of the hotel, Harvey Garrod with them. The latter had insisted on hearing what the sheriff had to say about the chase, saying he felt fine now.

'It was me who was robbed, remember,' Harvey said. 'I need to be kept in the picture.' But although he was relieved to hear that Pike's man had got clean away, he got a shock when he heard Doc McFee's only-too-accurate suspicions.

'The hotel robbery was a set-up,' the doc said to Floyd. 'OK, the owlhoot got away with a few hundred dollars, but that would be chickenfeed to what they took from the bank. Thousands rather than hundreds.'

' 'Xactly,' Floyd said. 'There was the miners' pay. More than six thousand, plus the bank's reserves.'

'So the hotel robber was a decoy!' Tom said. 'I knew it! He wanted us at least two hours away from Solace.'

'An' we fell for it,' Floyd agreed, bitterly.

'The last thing Arthur Makin said before he breathed his last sounded like "pipe",' Doc said. 'But I've been thinking – what if I misheard him? What if he actually said "*Pike*"?'

'Meaning the Pike gang?' Floyd said. 'You think Arthur recognized one of the raiders and was trying to point us in the right direction?'

'I just don't know,' Doc said. 'But it would explain why they had to kill him and Howie. The Pike gang don't leave witnesses.'

Harvey could feel his legs start to buckle and he sat down quickly.

'You OK, Harve?' Floyd said.

'Yes, yes, I'm fine.'

'Not that any of this is going to help us much now,' Doc went on. 'A dead witness – in this case *two* dead witnesses – never got anybody hanged.'

'True,' Floyd said. 'Seems like we're beat.'

'Meg came close to being caught up in the bank raid,' Chester told Tom, and went on to explain about her visit to the bank and the torn dress.

'Is she OK?' Tom wanted to know.

'Just a bit shaken, I reckon,' Chester said.

'I'm gonna go an' see her,' Tom said.

Chester smiled. 'Figured you would. I'll come with you. Seems to be nothing more any of us can do here.'

Meg had just finished changing her dress when Aunt

Carrie put her head round the door. The older woman was smiling.

'Tom's here, Meg,' she said. 'You decent?'

'Yes,' Meg replied. Her mind still on Clay, she wasn't sure she wanted to see Tom, afraid he would ask questions and then detect something in her manner.

'Then I'll tell him to come through.'

'It . . . it's all right, I'll come out.' Perhaps it would be easier not to see him alone, she thought.

Tom and her uncle were discussing the bank raid but stopped abruptly as she came through from her room. Tom saw her at that moment and hurried across to put an arm round her.

'You all right? Chester said you tore your dress outside the bank.'

'Y . . . yes,' Meg said. 'I tripped and fell against the hitching rail outside. There must have been a nail . . . anyway, it was too badly torn to go on, I had to come back.'

'Thank God for that,' Tom said, putting an arm round her shoulder. 'Those varmints could've shot you, the way they did Howie and Mr Makin.'

'Th. . .they're both dead?' Meg's voice was barely a whisper.

Tom nodded. 'You must've seen the gang's horses, if the men were still inside when you fell against the hitchin' rail. They would've been tied up there. Was there anythin' special about any of them? Somethin' that could help identify the rider?'

'N . . . no,' Meg said. 'I don't think so.'

'Could you hear anythin' of what was happenin' inside?'

'No, nothing,' Meg said. 'Not . . . not until I was more than halfway back across the street, then I heard some shots.'

'How many?'

'I don't know,' she said.

'OK,' Tom said. He frowned. 'Are you all right? You seem . . . worried about somethin'.'

'I'm fine, Tom,' Meg said quickly, forcing herself to smile. 'It's just all a bit of a shock, Howie and Mr Makin getting killed like that.'

'Why did the varmints have to do that?' Carrie said. 'Makes no sense.'

'We reckon Arthur Makin recognized one or more of them, even though they were masked, an' he was foolish enough to let 'em know that,' Tom explained.

Carrie nodded. 'That would be a mistake.'

CHAPTER
FOURTEEN

Harvey Garrod left Solace before first light the next morning and arrived in Weslake six hours later – mid-morning.

Harvey was angry. Angry because Nate Morgan had robbed him and knocked him out and taken his money, when all the man was supposed to have done was tie him up and *pretend* to take the hotel cash; and angry because Pike or one of his men had deemed it necessary to kill the bank manager and the teller. None of that had been part of the plan as Harvey had understood it when he had made the deal with Eli Pike.

Worse still, Sheriff Wickes was already half convinced it was the Pike gang who had been responsible for the robbery, thanks to Arthur Makin living long enough to point the finger at them. And now the chances were that Floyd or that over-eager young deputy would take it into their heads to try and do something about it, maybe start ferreting around for answers. Even discover Harvey's complicity in the crimes.

Jesus, it was a mess!

Which was why Harvey was now in Weslake, where he learned from the hotel clerk when he booked a room for the night that the Pike gang's hangout was a derelict ranch called the Lazy O, some two hours' buggy ride north of the town.

'Not that I'd recommend you going out there, unless you've got a really good reason,' the hotel clerk had said. 'They're a tough bunch, and they don't make visitors welcome.'

'Can't be helped,' Harvey had said.

In fact, there were two urgent reasons why he had to find Eli Pike before young Tom Walsh or Sheriff Wickes were able to confront the outlaw. One, he had to warn Eli about Makin's last words, and two, he had to get his daughter out of the gang's clutches.

He rode out of town, taking the main trail. Had he known there was a shorter route – an old Indian trail – he would have met Eli Pike coming *into* town and things might have turned out differently.

Back in Solace, Tom was sitting on the corner of Floyd's desk looking thoughtful. 'Mind you, Pike an' his men don't know that Arthur Makin might have named 'em before he died, do they?' he said. 'It's my bet whichever of 'em shot Mr Makin assumed they'd killed him outright.'

Floyd frowned. 'It's possible. What you gettin' at, Tom?'

'Well, just supposin' I was to go to Weslake first thing tomorrow – where everybody reckons the Pikes hang out from time to time – an' make folks, includin' the sheriff, believe that we have a *live* witness to the killin' of Howie an' Mr Makin, an' the robbin' of the bank. A witness who's willin' to name the Pikes as the guilty ones. Name 'em to the marshal or a circuit judge. Maybe then word will get back to the Pikes an' it'll scare Eli Pike or one of the others into comin' back to Solace to finish the job. An' we'll have them in our jurisdiction!'

'An' maybe you'll get yourself killed first off, Tom. The Pikes are jus' as likely to put a bullet in your back before comin' back here. Back-shootin's their style.'

'Then I'll jus' have to be careful,' Tom said.

'If anybody was to go, it should be me,' Floyd said.

'Aw, come on, Floyd!' Tom said. 'Give me a break. Let me do somethin' off my own bat for once.'

Floyd sighed. 'I jus' don't want you to go gettin' your-self killed. Good deputies ain't easy to find!'

Tom grinned. 'Nice to know I'm useful. Reckon I'll tell Meg what a rarity I am when I see her later.'

'Get out of here!' Floyd told him, laughing.

'They just didn't reckon on Mr Makin survivin' long enough to tell the doc anythin', so this might work.' Tom was telling his plan to Meg and the Greens that evening. 'Anyway, I plan to go to Weslake in the mornin', leave a coupl'a hours after sun-up. Weslake's where the Pikes sometimes hang out,' he explained.

'Oh, no, Tom!' Meg pleaded. 'It's too dangerous.'

'And to what purpose?' Carrie Green put in. 'Weslake's outside your jurisdiction and the Pikes are never going to admit it was them who robbed our bank, not now there *really are* no live . . . witnesses.' She glanced across at Meg.

Meg looked away, feeling her face getting hot.

She knows I've not told the truth.

'They can't be sure of that,' Tom said. 'An' I'm gonna let 'em believe either Howie or Mr Makin ain't dead, hopin' that'll scare 'em into doin' or sayin' somethin' stupid, somethin' incriminatin'. Better still, scare 'em into comin' back to Solace to finish the job, then Floyd an' me will have 'em.' He looked at Meg. 'Listen, I can't just sit back an' do nothin', Meg. Howie was a good friend of mine, an' I aim to get the man who killed him.'

And that man was Clay, thought Meg. *My own brother.*

CHAPTER FIFTEEN

Eli Pike was talking with Abe Lucre, Weslake's undertaker, arranging to have Silas buried the next day. Sheriff Cord Lewis hovered nearby.

'Just leave everythin' to me, Mr Pike,' Abe said.

The story Eli was telling everybody was that Silas had been killed by a stray bullet from a renegade bunch of Indians who had ambushed him at Checker Pass. The mortician didn't believe a word of it, and neither did Cord Lewis, but they pretended to swallow the tale. It never paid to argue with Eli Pike.

'You're sure gonna miss your brother, Eli,' Cord said. 'Indians, eh?'

'Yeah, Indians,' Eli repeated. He didn't care whether they believed him or not.

'Well, don't you worry,' Abe assured him. 'Silas'll get a good send-off.'

After leaving the undertakers, Eli headed to the saloon. Cord Lewis made as if to join him, but Eli waved him away.

'Not now, Cord.'

'Oh, sure, Eli.' The sheriff headed back to his office,

wondering how Silas Pike had *really* got himself killed. Some hold-up was his best guess.

Eli spent the next two hours sitting alone and drinking, still puzzled and enraged at the way a well-planned bank raid could have gone so badly wrong.

When he finally got back to the ranch, it was late evening. He was surprised to find Harvey Garrod waiting for him, and even more surprised to see Becky standing with her father.

'So the cat's out of the bag,' he said, looking at Becky. 'Now you know about the *arrangement* between your pa an' me.'

Becky nodded, a mixture of fear and hope etched on her face. 'An' I want to go home with him,' she said. 'Please, Eli!'

'Shut up!' Eli yelled at her. 'Nobody's goin' anywhere!'

Harvey put an arm round his daughter's shoulders. 'Her release in exchange for getting the sheriff, the deputy and half the town out of Solace before the bank raid,' he said. 'That was the deal, Pike, and I kept my end of it.'

Nate, Ray and Clay were sitting around the room, which, Eli guessed, was the only reason Garrod hadn't taken his daughter and gone. They would have stopped him. The saddle-bags, still unpacked and bulky with the cash from the bank, had been slung into the corner of the room the night before. Somehow, none of them had had the inclination to count up the booty until today. And even then, Ray, Clay and Nate had decided to await Eli's return from the undertaker's in Weslake before opening the saddle-bags. It was an unspoken rule that they never divided up the spoils from any robbery without Eli being present.

'You're damn prompt, Garrod!' Eli said now, his voice thick with the effects of alcohol and fatigue. It had been a long twenty-four hours, in which things had gone sour and he had lost a brother. He was in no mood for arguing. 'An' how did you know you'd find me here?'

'I asked around in Weslake,' Harvey said.

Eli nodded. 'Guessed so. Folks are gettin' too damn talkative in that town. Were you reckonin' on takin' missy with you tonight? 'Cause if you were, you can forget it.'

'But you promised! You gave me your word!' The desperation in Harvey's voice was palpable. 'That was the arrangement and . . .'

'Yeah, well, I've changed my mind.' Eli glanced at the others. 'We're buryin' Silas tomorrow. Then we start packin' up. We're gettin' out of here.' He looked back at Garrod. 'Becky's comin' with us.'

There was a sharp gasp from the girl as her father drew her closer to him. 'No!' he said. 'I won't have that!'

'Please, Eli!' Becky pleaded.

'It ain't up for discussion,' Eli said.

He nodded at Nate and Ray and the two men moved across the room and prised Becky away from her father. She screamed and Harvey tried to put up a fight, but Ray hit him across the mouth, then twice into the soft flesh of his belly, leaving him doubled over and gasping for breath.

'Take the girl upstairs,' Eli ordered Nate.

'*Pa!*' Becky screamed, as Nate dragged her towards the stairwell.

Eli looked across at Clay. 'Put Mr Garrod in his buggy

an' send him on his way, kid. Any trouble, kill him.'

Clay, who had been watching Becky with a sick feeling in his gut, nodded, took his .45 from his holster and pushed the older man outside to the echoes of his daughter's screams. Garrod was distraught, taking gulps of breath and clutching his stomach.

When they were some yards from the house, Clay made a decision. He lowered his voice and said, 'Don't worry about Becky. I'll see she's OK. I aim to get away an' take her with me.'

Harvey stared at him at him in astonishment. When he found his voice, it was more with disgust than appreciation that he said, 'So that she can spend the rest of her life with you – a *gunslinger*? Never! I want her home with me.' He climbed into his buggy, trying to reclaim some of his dignity. 'This isn't over. I'm getting help, even if I do have to own up to my part in the hotel robbery and the bank raid.'

Clay watched Harvey Garrod drive away from the Lazy O as a cloud passed across the face of the moon. Then he turned to see Ray standing just a few yards behind him.

Had the other man overheard him speaking to Garrod?

'Get your horse an' come with me, kid,' Ray said. 'There's a bit of clearin' up to do, especially after what Garrod just said. Can't have him shootin' his mouth off.'

'Where are we going?' Clay asked, although he had already guessed.

Ray nodded towards Harvey Garrod's retreating back. 'We're goin' after him, before he can cause any more trouble. He knows too much and Eli wants him dead. We'll take the Indian trail an' cut him off at Checker Pass. We can be there a good fifteen minutes ahead of him. Come on, before he gets too much of a head start.'

'Wh . . . why d'you need me?' Clay said. The last thing he wanted was any part in killing Becky's father. 'It don't take two to. . . .'

'We've got some talkin' to do,' Ray cut in. 'Remember?'

Clay swallowed. 'OK.'

They took the old Indian trail, riding fast, their horses kicking up the dirt. The moon cut shafts of light between the trees. Questions about how much Ray knew whirled in Clay's head, but neither man spoke on the journey.

Fifteen minutes later they emerged from a stand of pine trees on to a long, high ridge, finally drawing their horses to a halt behind a formation of boulders. The animals were breathing heavily.

Clay tried to ignore the sick feeling in the pit of his stomach. He had killed two more men since that first cat-astrophic accident in the saloon at Adam's Creek, and now he was going be a witness to another slaying.

Well, whatever happened afterwards, he had come to a decision. He was finished with Eli and the others. When they left the next day, he wouldn't be going with them. He'd had enough. It was time to do something about his life. Maybe there was some way that he and his sister could. . . .

'What's on your mind, kid?' Ray said, interrupting Clay's musings.

'You didn't need me to come with you,' Clay said. 'Didn't Eli ask why you were takin' me?'

'I told him I was takin' you for back-up,' Ray told him.

'Did he believe you?'

Ray shrugged. 'Who knows? You can never tell with Eli. He didn't argue. He just wants Garrod out of the way.'

'Eli double-crossed him,' Clay said.

Ray shrugged. 'That's about it.'

They were silent for some moments, then Clay said, 'So what did you want to talk to me about? Why did you bring me? It doesn't need two of us.'

'I know that you killed Silas,' Ray said.

Clay stared at him. 'How . . . how d'you know?'

'The bank teller's six-gun,' Ray said. 'I picked it up afore we left. It was cold an' fully loaded. *He* didn't kill Silas.' He stared at Clay: 'It was you, wasn't it, kid?'

Clay nodded after a moment. 'Yeah, but I had to do it. I had no choice.'

'What 'xactly happened? Somethin' to do with that female scream I heard, the one you tried to pass off as havin' come from the bank teller? Horseshit!'

'It . . . it was my sister who screamed,' Clay admitted. 'She came into the bank while you an' Eli were with the bank manager, gettin' the money from the safe.'

'Your *sister*?'

'Yeah, it was a real shock, believe me. I reckon she lives in Solace now, which prob'ly means my pa is dead.' Clay said, absently rubbing the knife scar on his forehead.

'So what happened? Go on.'

'Silas started pawin' her,' Clay said. 'Tore her dress open an' touched her . . . anyways I told him to quit, but he wouldn't. So I . . . I had to kill him.'

'An' the teller?'

'He drew a gun an' I had to kill him, too, afore he killed

me,' Clay answered. 'So then I lied an' told Eli the teller killed Silas.'

Ray looked thoughtful. 'When we saw Silas' body, his face was uncovered.'

'His neckerchief slipped, yeah,' Clay said.

'So there's a witness – your sister. A live witness who can describe him,' Ray said. 'Which means the Solace sheriff will show her a few law dodgers, an' in no time he'll know it was Eli Pike an' his gang who robbed the local bank.'

'Meg won't say anythin', 'cause of me,' Clay said.

Ray shook his head. 'Can't be sure of that. It's too much of a risk. Eli will want her dead afore she gets a chance to tell some marshal or testify to a circuit judge. I'll have to tell Eli.'

'*No! You can't tell him!*' Panic flooded through Clay like a tidal wave.

The other man shrugged. 'I have to . . .' He stopped abruptly at the sound of an approaching horse and buggy. 'He's comin',' he said.

There was enough light for them to see the main trail as the buggy moved towards them at a canter, Harvey Garrod's rotund figure silhouetted by the moonlight as it drew nearer.

Ray, sitting astride his horse, lifted his Winchester and took aim. But luck was on the hotel owner's side. At the moment Ray fired, Garrod's horse swerved to avoid a pothole, and the bullet missed the hotelier by inches.

Ray swore.

The sound of the shot also spooked the horse, which reared up, bucking the buggy so that Harvey was thrown out.

Ray leapt from his own horse and half ran, half slithered down the slope towards the buggy.

Harvey rolled over in the dirt, scrambled to his feet and ran for cover behind a bush, pulling his .45 from the holster under his frock coat. He rarely carried a firearm, but had felt the need of one before confronting Eli Pike. Much good it had done him at the ranch, he'd reflected as he'd driven away. Now, however, it might be all that was between him and a bloody death.

Instinctively and without taking aim, he fired twice – and was astonished to see that luck must again have been on his side. One of his bullets seemed to have found its mark on the outlaw as the latter staggered and fell. Harvey scrambled to his feet and stumbled towards the buggy. But this time his luck ran out. Ray eased himself up from the ground, lifted his Winchester and fired, then fell back into the dirt. His bullet blew a hole in Harvey's forehead.

Clay's hand was shaking. He reholstered his .45, swallowed the bile in his throat and jumped from his horse. He slithered down the slope to Ray and saw the older man's face drained of blood. Clay dropped to his knees beside him.

'Garrod got lucky with his shot,' he said.

'No, kid,' Ray said, choking on the words. 'Garrod . . . couldn't shoot straight to . . . save his life.' His clouded eyes stared straight at Clay, his voice weakening by the second. '*But you can . . . an' you did.* Right?'

Clay avoided the dying man's eye. 'Yeah,' he admitted eventually. 'Couldn't let you tell Eli about Meg.'

A trickle of blood seeped from the corner of the other man's mouth as he spoke.

'Should've guessed . . . you'd have to finish me off to keep me quiet . . . You need to . . . get your sister away, kid, afore Eli finds out the truth . . . an. . . .'

His face creased with a sudden spasm of pain and his eyes opened wide for a second before freezing into a sightless stare.

'*Sheeit*!' Clay swore. 'What am I gonna tell Eli?' He looked down at Harvey Garrod's body. 'Gotta do somethin' about him, too. An' the horse an' buggy. Can't just leave things as they are.'

The temptation was to simply ride off somewhere, as far away from Eli Pike and the Lazy O as he could get. But high-tailing it meant abandoning both Meg and Becky, and somehow he just couldn't do that.

So he had to clean things up here, and go back.

CHAPTER SIXTEEN

Eli Pike poured himself a shot of whiskey, then passed the bottle to Nate. They sat on either side of the table ruminating over the bank robbery and how things had gone wrong. They still hadn't counted the take from the raid.

Becky had gone to bed soon after her pa had left the ranch, overcome with feelings of despair. Would her father get help and come back? But who would help him? He had told nobody in Solace of her predicament, she was sure of that.

'How much money did you get from Garrod's safe at the hotel?' Eli asked Nate. 'You never said. An' I'm guessin' it was more'n the few dollars Garrod planned for you to take, right?'

Nate shrugged. 'Few more, yeah. He tried hidin' it, but not very well.'

'So how much?'

'Coupl'a hundred dollars.'

Eli gave a short laugh. 'It's OK. You can keep it. You prob'ly earned it, layin' that trail for the posse to follow.'

He stopped at the sound of a fast-approaching rider

101

and both men rose from the table. Minutes later, Clay burst through the door.

One look at the youngster's face told Eli something was wrong. 'Where's Ray?' he demanded.

'Dead. Garrod managed to get him with a lucky bullet,' Clay told him, and gave a fictitious summary of the events at Checker Pass, excluding his own part in the proceedings.

'Hell an' damnation!' Eli slammed a fist down on the porch rail.

'At least Garrod won't be doin' any talkin',' Nate said.

'What're we gonna tell Becky, Eli?' Clay asked.

'What I was plannin' to tell her,' Eli said. 'That you an' Ray went after her pa to try an' calm him down. That he pulled a gun on you an' Ray shot him in self-defence.'

'She gonna believe that?'

'If anythin', it'll sound even more believable now Ray's dead,' Eli said. 'Did you leave the bodies at the Pass?'

Clay nodded. 'Pulled 'em into the mesquite an' covered 'em with brush,' he said, trying to keep his voice steady. 'Thought it best not to bring the bodies back in case I got seen. An' it was too dark to bury 'em. Anyways, didn't 'ave nothin' to bury 'em with. Hid Garrod's buggy well off the trail. Be a while afore anybody finds anythin'.'

'The horses?' Eli said.

'Turned the horse from the buggy loose. Brought Ray's back with me. Brought his saddle and guns back, too.'

Eli nodded slowly, thinking. 'You did good, kid. Reckon I'll get Cord Lewis to get rid of the bodies tomorrow. He an' a couple of his men. Cord'll pay 'em to keep their mouths shut.'

Clay could feel Nate's eyes on him as he told his story. Why was he looking suspicious? Surely he didn't think that he, Clay, had killed Ray?

I've got to get away, he thought.

CHAPTER SEVENTEEN

Mid-morning the following day, after a hard six-hour ride from Solace, Tom was riding up the main street of Weslake.

A quick survey of the town's buildings identified the sheriff's office, and he made his way there. He was dismounting from his horse by the hitch rail when an old-timer who was sitting in a chair on the boardwalk spoke to him.

'If'n you're lookin' for the sheriff, he ain't there,' he said. He was building a smoke, and barely glanced at Tom. 'Rode out of town with Jed Dell an' Harry Tiler. Didn't say where they were goin', but reckon they were on Pike business.'

'Pike business?' Tom queried. 'You talkin' about Eli Pike?'

The old man nodded. 'The very same. Pike came to see Cord earlier. Saw 'em talkin' together. Cord an' his buddies left soon after.'

'Cord?' Tom said.

'Cord Lewis, that's the sheriff.' He gave a derisory snort and finished making his cigarette. 'Well, that's what he calls himself. "Pike's yes-man" 'd be a better description.'

'Any idea where they were headin'?' Tom asked the garrulous old-timer.

'Nope. Don't ask questions no more. Healthier that way, 'specially where the Pikes are concerned. Although there's only one Pike to worry about now, which is somethin' of a blessin' for the town.'

'Only one Pike?'

'Yep. Silas is dead.'

Tom digested this new piece of information.

'Anyway, thanks,' he said. 'Guess I'll stable my horse. There a livery near here?'

The old-timer nodded towards the other end of the street. 'You plannin' on stayin' awhile?'

'Yeah,' Tom said.

'Where you from?'

Tom laughed. 'Thought you didn't ask questions.'

The old man scowled. 'Jus' curious. Name's Smokey Harrison.'

'Tom Walsh,' Tom told him. 'From Solace. We had us a bank robbery an' I'm followin' up a lead.'

'You the law there?' Smokey asked, noting the absence of a badge on Tom's shirt.

'Deputy sheriff,' Tom admitted after a moment.

'Kinda strayed outside your jurisdiction, ain't you, kid?'

'Guess I have,' Tom said.

Smokey's eyes narrowed. 'Bank robbery, you say. Anybody get hurt?'

Tom nodded. 'Bank teller an' the manager.'

'Dead?'

Tom hesitated. 'Yeah,' he said. 'But I'd be glad if'n you'd keep that bit of information to yourself.'

Smokey Harrison puffed on his cigarette and looked thoughtful. 'Let me see if I can figure this out,' he said. 'You had a bank robbery. The "lead" you mentioned brought you to Weslake where the Pike gang hang out. So it's likely you reckon they're responsible – an' I ain't gonna argue with you.'

'Go on, old-timer,' Tom said.

'Maybe you have a witness – or had a witness, but he's dead now,' Smokey continued, after puffing on his cigarette. He studied Tom carefully before a half-smile spread across his face. 'Yeah, he's dead but you want Eli Pike to think you've got a *live* witness. That about right, lawman?'

Tom smiled. 'You're no fool, Smokey.'

'Jus' 'cause a fellah's old, don't mean he's dumb,' Smokey said. 'Truth is, I was a lawman myself once. It's the smart kinda ploy I'd have thought up, too.' He nodded towards the empty sheriff's office. 'But if you were hopin' to get some help from him in there, you're gonna be disappointed. Cord Lewis is little more than Eli Pike's lackey.'

'So I've heard,' Tom said.

'Tell me somethin',' Smokey said. 'Did any of the gang get killed in your bank robbery?'

'Yeah,' Tom said. 'One did.'

Smokey nodded slowly. 'Figures,' he said.

'How'd you mean?'

'Silas Pike's funeral's later today,' Smokey said. 'Word is, he was killed in an ambush by some renegade Indians out near Checker Pass coupl'a days ago. Horseshit! Ain't been an Indian in this territory for years. But you don't question Eli Pike. Not if you wanna stay healthy.'

'Interestin',' Tom said. 'Where's the funeral gonna be?'

'Boot Hill.' Smokey said. 'Half a mile outside of town, headin' north. You plannin' on puttin' in an appearance?'

'Reckon I might at that,' Tom said.

'Watch your back,' Smokey told him. 'Eli Pike don't like strangers. Tends to shoot first an' ask questions after.'

'I aim to be extra careful,' Tom said.

CHAPTER EIGHTEEN

Carrie Green watched Meg as she finished serving the woman who had come in for a length of calico and some ribbon. Although the girl was her usual polite self, she seemed preoccupied – worried even. After the woman had left and the store was empty of customers, Carrie walked across to the door, turned the key and pulled down the wicker blind.

Meg looked at her in surprise. 'Are we closing?' she asked. It was mid-day.

Carrie came back and leaned her elbows on the counter, looking at her niece. 'Chester's gone for his haircut,' she said. 'And now we've the place to ourselves for a while, Meg. So, are you going to tell me the truth about how your dress got torn? And please don't insult my intelligence with that story about a hitching rail and a nail. Chester may have swallowed it, but I haven't.'

Meg's face coloured.

'You went *into* the bank, didn't you?' her aunt persisted.

After a moment, Meg nodded. 'Yes.'

'So tell me what happened. One of those varmints tear your dress?'

There seemed no point in denying it, so Meg nodded again. 'He . . . touched me.' She put a hand on her breast.

Carrie Green nodded slowly, as if finally having had her worst suspicions confirmed. 'Oh, my darling!' she said. 'What did you do . . . I mean, how did you stop him from. . . . ?'

'Clay stopped him,' Meg said, softly. She was suddenly relieved to be able to tell someone. The lie she had been giving out had weighed heavily on her conscience.

'*Clay*?' Carrie gasped. 'Your *brother*? He was part of the gang?'

'He seemed to be,' Meg admitted.

Carrie was silent for several moments as she digested this astonishing piece of information. But the more she thought about it, the less astonishing it appeared.

'Clay was always a burden to my brother Matthew. Wild and wayward, and in all probability responsible for Matthew's declining health and premature death. That's Chester's opinion, too.' She put a hand on Meg's arm. 'So, what did Clay do to stop the man. . . ?'

'Shot him,' Meg said quickly. 'And . . . and then he shot Howie Clark when Howie pulled a gun on him.'

Carrie closed her eyes. 'Have mercy on us,' she said.

Tears sprang unbidden into Meg's eyes. 'And now Tom's gone to Weslake hoping to mete out some kind of justice on the Pike gang. Which will include my brother. Except that Tom doesn't know he's my brother.'

'And if they meet up, Clay won't know Tom's your fiancé,' Carrie said.

'Which makes everything even worse,' Meg said, sobbing.

'Maybe somebody should put both of them in the picture,' Carrie said.

Meg stared at her. 'Who?'

'Sheriff Wickes. You've got to tell him what happened at the bank.'

'I . . . I can't!' Meg said.

Carrie put a hand on Meg's arm. 'You've got to go and tell him exactly what you've told me, my dear. The whole story.'

'But . . .'

There was a rattling at the door as someone tried to enter. Carrie frowned and went across. She lifted the blind an inch or two before unlocking the door.

'It's Chester,' she said. 'And when he hears what you've got to say, I know he's going to agree with me.'

Meg sighed and put her head in her hands.

Twenty minutes later, sitting across from the sheriff in his office, Meg once again recounted her story.

'Your *brother*?' Floyd said, after she had finished.

Meg nodded.

'You've never mentioned that you had a brother,' Floyd said.

'I . . . I thought it best not to,' she said. She looked directly at Floyd. 'Especially not to a sheriff, seeing that Clay was wanted by the law and his face is probably on one of those law dodgers in your desk.'

'An' especially as you're plannin' to marry my deputy,' Floyd said.

Meg's face coloured. She nodded.

'But how did your brother get hooked up with Pike's gang?'

'I don't know,' Meg said. 'And now Tom's gone after Clay and the others without knowing who Clay is.'

'Then your aunt's right. I reckon somebody'd better go to Weslake an' tell him, otherwise you could end up with a dead brother. Or a dead husband-to-be.'

Floyd rose from his chair and looked at the clock on the wall behind his desk. 'If I leave now, I should be there by nightfall.'

CHAPTER NINETEEN

Tom stabled his horse at the livery, then took a room at the Weslake Hotel. Afterwards he found a café and ordered a plate of bacon, beans and potatoes from the Chinese waiter. He washed this down with three mugs of strong coffee, then built himself a smoke.

He was conscious of being eyed with curiosity by the handful of other diners, and at the star-shaped badge Tom had decided to pin back on to his shirt. He gave friendly acknowledgement to their glances but none seemed anxious to make his acquaintance.

A little before two o'clock he looked out of the café window and noticed a small, slow-moving procession of people following a black wooden hearse, pulled by a black horse and bearing a coffin. The mourners walked behind it, led by a tall, lean man, somewhere in his thirties, with a heavy drooping moustache. Eli Pike, Tom presumed. He'd seen the man's image on a law dodger. Walking a step or two behind Eli was a young woman and three more men. Tom couldn't see the woman's face, which was shrouded in a drooping hat and black veil, but he sensed something familiar about her gait.

He waited until they were at the edge of town before leaving the café and following them up a sloping path to the graveyard. He saw Smokey Harrison watching him from his chair on the boardwalk.

Tom stood amongst the gravestones, a short distance from the little gathering, as the preacher performed the burial ceremony. He watched Eli Pike, the young woman, and the two men next to her. A little to one side was Cord Lewis, the sheriff, easily identified by his badge of office. The two men next to the girl, Tom guessed, were Eli Pike's associates. One, the meanest-looking, with a face devoid of any expression and wearing a brown riding duster and black hat, was about Eli Pike's age. The other, a short, stocky fellow, was a good few years younger, probably not yet twenty. Tom wondered which of these had shot Howie and the bank manager?

One other thing puzzled him. From the accounts given after the robbery, one or two Solace townsfolk had been able to give rough descriptions of the three men who had ridden away, one of whom seemed older than the other two. So where was he? Back at Pike's ranch?

The coffin having been interred and the last few words spoken by the preacher, the little group turned and began walking back down the path towards the town. The preacher remained at the graveside, as if wishing to disassociate himself from any further proceedings.

As he watched them, Tom saw the young woman lift the veil away from her face – and felt a jolt of recognition.

Becky Garrod!

What in blazes was she doing with the Pike gang?

113

Wasn't she supposed to be with some aunt up north? That was the story Harvey Garrod was telling at any rate. Did the Solace hotel owner know his daughter was mixed up with a bunch of desperados? Surely not. Although . . . the hotel robbery. . . .

A thought struck Tom like a lightning bolt. *Could Harvey Garrod have been part of the decoy plan?*

The little group was suddenly level with Tom, and he stepped forwards.

'Howdy, Becky,' he said.

The phalanx of mourners came to a halt, each individual staring at the interloper. Becky looked both startled and fearful. She opened her mouth to say something, but closed it again as Eli put a hand on her arm. He looked first at Tom's face, then at his badge, then at his face again.

'You know this lawman, Cord?' he asked, his gaze remaining on Tom.

'Nope, Eli,' the sheriff answered. 'Never seen him afore.'

'Becky?' Eli asked.

When the girl replied, her voice was an unsteady whisper. 'His name's Tom Walsh. He's deputy sheriff at Solace.'

Eli affected an interested expression. 'That so? What brings you to Weslake, mister deputy? An' what's your interest in my brother's funeral?'

'There was a bank robbery in Solace two days ago,' Tom said, keeping his voice matter-of-fact in an attempt to conceal his nervousness. 'A man was killed. The other *witness* . . .' he laid emphasis on the word '. . . the other witness has named the Pike gang as the perpetrators of the crime.'

114

' "Perpetrators",' Eli mimicked. 'That's a fine two-dollar word, mister. Well, your *witness* must be mistaken. Me an' my friends here – if you insist on callin' us a *gang* – were at my ranch all day that day, ain't that right, Becky?'

The girl swallowed and nodded.

'In fact, Sheriff Lewis here was with us most of the day too, ain't that right, Cord?' Pike stared directly at the sheriff.

'Y-yeah, that's a fact, Eli.' Cord Lewis avoided the other man's eye.

'So you see, Mr Walsh, your witness is kind'a confused.' Eli Pike's expression changed to one of displeasure and his voice rose several decibels. 'Now, I'll thank you to leave me to mourn my brother's passin' in peace. An' I suggest you take yourself back to Solace, *you hear?*'

Tom held his gaze. 'Your brother not with you two days ago then?' he said after a moment.

'Eh? What?' Eli looked momentarily confused.

'Heard he was killed by a bunch of renegade Indians at about that time,' Tom said, calmly. 'Did I get that wrong?'

Eli moved closer, his eyes ablaze with fury. When he spoke his voice was laced with cold venom. 'I'll tell you what you got wrong, mister lawman. Comin' here, *that's* what you got wrong. Take my advice an' get back to Solace, lessen you want more trouble than you can handle.'

With that, he pushed past Tom and marched on down the path. Tom watched them.

At one point Becky Garrod glanced back, her face a picture of dread.

CHAPTER TWENTY

'Get rid of the lawman,' Eli told Nate. 'If he ain't left for Solace by nightfall, make sure he can't go anywhere.'

They were standing outside the undertaker's office. Several yards away, Becky was sitting in the buggy Eli had used to drive them both into town. Cord Lewis was walking back to his office. Clay had headed towards the Holed Ace saloon.

Nate nodded. He watched Eli join Becky in the buggy and drive away, then followed Clay. He caught up with the youngster at the bar.

'You believe that lawman?' Clay asked him. He was nursing a whiskey and looked nervous.

'About what?' Nate said.

'You reckon he was tellin' the truth about a witness at the bank?'

Nate shrugged. 'You were there, kid.'

'I shot the teller,' Clay admitted. 'I saw Eli shoot the manager. You reckon one of them survived the shootin'?'

'Maybe. Or maybe the lawman's bluffin',' Nate said, waving to the barkeep for a whiskey. 'Ain't important. Eli's told me to get rid of him if'n he ain't headin' for Solace by nightfall.'

'That don't solve the problem of the witness, if there is one,' Clay said.

'Nope.' Nate removed his knife from its sheath inside his boot and began paring his fingernails.

'So?'

'So I guess we'll just have to wait an' see,' Nate said. He looked across to the stairs where two saloon girls were sitting. One of them caught Nate's eye and looked questioningly at him. He gave a half-smile and re-sheathed his knife. 'See you later, kid,' he said. 'Got some company to keep.' He downed his drink and walked towards the girl.

Clay watched them ascend the stairs, then signalled to the barkeep to bring him the bottle. He was worried. Too worried to enjoy the delights of one of the saloon girls. Could the lawman's 'witness' be Meg, and not one of the two bank staff? Had Meg worked out that it was the Pike gang he was mixed up with? Even if she had, he found it hard to believe she would tell the law and put him in danger. He was her *brother*, dammit! He'd stopped Silas mauling her and he'd let her go! And had she figured out that Becky Garrod was with the gang? Silas had mentioned the name. Clay poured himself another drink with a shaking hand.

'You were at the funeral,' a voice said from behind him.

Clay swivelled round and almost fell off the bar stool when he saw the Solace deputy at his shoulder. 'Go away, mister,' he said. 'I ain't got nothin' to say to you.'

'Really? That's too bad. The name's Walsh, by the way. You got a name?'

117

Clay swallowed a mouthful of his drink before answering. 'Ain't none of your business.'

Tom Walsh shrugged. 'Makes no difference. I can always ask around.'

'It's Thornton! That satisfy you?' The words were out of Clay's mouth before the appalling significance of what he'd let slip by revealing his real name dawned on him. Did the man know Meg?

Tom was frowning. 'Thornton?'

It seemed he did.

'Y . . . yeah, what about it?' Clay tried to sound indifferent.

'Nothin',' Tom answered. Then asked, 'You got any kin?'

Clay shook his head. 'Nope. Now, why don't you get lost!'

'Just a coincidence, I guess.'

'Coincidence?'

'Yeah,' Tom said. 'My fiancée's name's Thornton. Meg Thornton.'

Clay swallowed. 'Your . . . fiancée?' He took another drink. 'Well, she ain't no kin of mine.'

The barkeep came across and Tom asked for a beer. He waited until it had been poured before speaking again. 'You're hooked up with Eli Pike.' It wasn't a question.

'I work for Mr Pike, yeah,' Clay said. 'Help out at the Lazy O.'

'So you know Becky Garrod.'

'Sure. She an' Mr Pike are . . . together,' Clay said.

'How did that come about?'

Clay shrugged. 'Can't remember.'

'I'm bettin' he treats her badly,' Tom said. 'Knocks her around. Am I right?'

Clay didn't reply. The whiskey was making his head fuzzy.

Tom swallowed some of his beer. 'What's your first name?'

Clay looked at him. 'Why?'

'Just wonderin'. Mine's Tom.'

'It's Clay,' Clay said after a moment. There seemed little point maintaining the 'Chet Adams' fiction.

'Listen, Clay,' Tom said. 'I came here to nail Eli Pike an' his gang for the killings at the Solace bank, an' I still aim to do that. But now there's somethin' else I need to do, an' that's to get Becky Garrod back to her pa. I'm pretty sure he don't know she's hooked up with Eli Pike or he'd have tried to do somethin' about it.'

Clay said nothing, picturing Harvey Garrod's body buried somewhere out near Checker Pass by Cord Lewis and his men earlier that day. Becky was never going to see her pa again, and she knew that. But maybe this lawman could get her away from Pike. Get her away from the Lazy O. For that, Clay would be grateful. He was slowly beginning to realize he'd never be able to do it on his own. And then he could concentrate on getting himself away from Eli and the remnants of the Pike gang.

But he was still trying to come to terms with the fact that the deputy was *engaged* to Meg, and that he didn't seem to know Meg had a brother who was part of the Pike gang. That she had a brother at all. Clearly Meg hadn't told him.

But what was she doing now, back in Solace? Fretting that her fiancé was going to discover the truth – that it was

119

her brother who had shot Silas and the bank teller?

He was conscious of Walsh watching him, and tried to act unconcerned.

'How're you gonna manage that? Becky sticks pretty close to Eli, he makes sure of that.'

Tom Walsh smiled. 'So you wouldn't warn Eli if I tried to make a move? That's interestin'. Maybe you could get a message to her.'

Clay glanced at the ceiling. In one of the rooms up there, Nate Morgan was enjoying the delights of one of the saloon whores, but his next job was to kill Walsh if the lawman hadn't left Weslake by nightfall. Clay tried to think a way round the dilemma.

'A message to Becky?' Tom prompted.

'I dunno,' Clay said. Nate would be coming down again soon and he didn't want to be seen talking with Walsh. 'I – I can't talk about it here.'

Tom had seen him look up at the ceiling. 'Worried about your friend? Oh, I saw him with you at the bar afore he went upstairs with the bar girl. OK, meet me back of the hotel in an hour. We can talk again.'

'No!' Clay said. 'Leave it until after dark. Say, nine o'clock.'

The deputy swallowed the remainder of his beer. 'OK, I'll be waitin'.' He nodded to the whiskey bottle. 'And I'd lay off any more of that stuff. Best to keep a clear head.' With that he slid himself off the bar stool and walked out through the batwings without looking back.

Clay saw that the hand holding his shot glass was shaking. What was he doing, palling up with a lawman who could get him hanged? Answer: because he saw a chance of helping Becky get away.

And because Walsh was Meg's husband-to-be?

That was another thing. How would she feel if he allowed Walsh to be gunned down without doing anything to stop it? Suddenly, Clay knew he couldn't let that happen.

'Jeeze, what a mess!' he muttered to himself.

CHAPTER
TWENTY-ONE

An hour later, Nate Morgan, his thirst for fornication quenched, came down the stairs and looked round the saloon. The kid had left, he noted, or was availing himself of one of the other whores. There was no sign of the Solace deputy either.

Question was, had the Solace lawman left town? Had he, Nate, been saved the task of killing him? Cord Lewis would know. Best pay him a visit.

The sheriff was sitting at his desk playing solitaire when Nate opened the door of his office. He looked up as Nate came in – and immediately dropped the cards. Nate made him nervous. There was something menacing about the way his eyes seemed to bore right into your soul as he looked at you. He would be a difficult man to lie to.

'That lawman left town yet?' Nate asked.

'He hadn't when I checked fifteen minutes ago.' Cord

avoided the other man's stare. 'I went to the livery an' his horse was still there. An' he hasn't checked out of the hotel. The clerk seemed to think he was stayin' overnight. Maybe he'll leave in the mornin'.'

'Nope,' Nate muttered to himself. 'Reckon he'll be stayin' here permanently.'

'What you say, Nate?' the sheriff asked.

'Nothin',' Nate said. And he turned and left, leaving the door open.

The sheriff watched him walk away down the street, leading the piebald. 'Gonna be trouble,' he muttered to himself.

Tom found Smokey Harrison in the café, tucking into a plate of beef stew.

'Mind if I join you?' Tom asked the old-timer. Smokey pointed to a chair with his fork. 'Help yourself.'

Tom looked across at the Chinese waiter and indicated that he'd have the same as Smokey. The Chinaman nodded briefly and disappeared into the kitchen.

'Know anythin' about the girl who's livin' with the Pike gang?' Tom asked Smokey. 'Her name's Becky Garrod.'

'What about her?'

'I'm wantin' to know how she came to get hooked up with Eli Pike.'

'You know her?' Smokey asked.

'Yeah,' Tom said. 'Her pa owns the Palace Hotel in Solace.'

'The story goes she joined up with Eli after a stage hold-up,' Smokey said. 'Seems she was a passenger an' she elected to go with Eli rather than go on to wherever it was

123

she an' the stage was headin'. I say "elected to go", but I'm guessin' Eli kinda insisted. When Eli wants somethin' he just goes ahead an' takes it, 'specially if it happens to be a pretty girl.'

Tom nodded. 'Kind'a adds up,' he said. 'She always was a reckless kid, lookin' for excitement an' often findin' she'd bit off more'n she could chew. Pike prob'ly didn't have to do much persuadin', although I'm bettin' she's lived to regret it.'

'Reckon she has,' Smokey said. 'She always looks like a scared rabbit whenever she's in town with Pike. Carries a few bruises, too.'

'That's what I figured,' Tom said. 'Can't believe her pa hasn't tried to find her afore now.'

Smokey put down his fork and pushed his empty plate aside. 'What's her pa look like?' he asked, suddenly interested.

'About fifty,' Tom said. 'Fat, with greyin' hair. Always wears a suit with a frock coat.'

'Drives a smart-lookin' buggy?' Smokey asked.

'Yeah,' Tom said.

'Reckon I might've seen him,' Smokey said.

'*Here*, in Weslake?'

'Reckon so. Early yesterday mornin'. He was askin' around about the Pikes' hangout.'

'*Yesterday mornin'*!'

'You sound surprised.'

'Damn right I am,' Tom said, thinking, *Floyd and me should've kept an eye on Harvey Garrod. A few things about the hotel robbery are beginning to add up.*

The Chinaman arrived at the table and placed a plate

124

of beef stew and a mug of coffee in front of Tom before moving away. Tom ignored it, staring into space.

'The thing is, Garrod's hotel safe was robbed just hours afore the bank raid,' Tom told the old-timer. 'Upshot of that was that me, the sheriff, an' most of the town's men were out of town when the bank raid happened, chasin' after the man who robbed the hotel.'

'You catch him?' Smokey asked.

Tom shook his head. 'Way we see it now, he made sure we followed him until we were two hours out of Solace, then wiped his trail.'

'So the hotel robbery was to lure you out of town,' Smokey said. 'The guy was a decoy.'

'Sure seems like it,' Tom said.

'Sounds like Nate Morgan,' Smokey said. 'Ain't the first time the Pikes have played that ruse usin' Nate. 'Course it means they have to have help from somebody willin' to be "robbed".'

Tom nodded. 'An' now you're tellin' me Harvey Garrod has been askin' about the home of Eli Pike. Eli Pike, who's got Harvey's daughter, an' whose gang robbed the bank at Solace.'

'An' you're thinkin' that this man Garrod did a *deal* with Eli Pike, that right?'

'Reckon he agreed to provide a reason to send our posse on a wild goose chase in exchange for Pike allowin' his daughter to go free,' Tom agreed. He frowned. 'Only that ain't happened so far. She was at Silas Pike's funeral, lookin' as scared as hell.'

'Wouldn't put it past Eli to double-cross this fellah Garrod,' Smokey said. ' 'Specially if'n he's taken a real fancy to the girl. An' if that's so, it's gonna be a real tough job to get her away.'

'Yeah, I guess you're right.' Tom forked up a mouthful of beef stew. 'Still, I may have got myself some help. Kid called Clay Thornton, one of Eli's gang.'

'The kid?' Smokey said. 'He's new. Only hooked up with Eli an' the others a few months ago. 'Ceptin' I thought his name was Adams. Chet Adams.'

'Even so, my guess is he's not happy about the way Eli treats Becky,' Tom said. 'Prob'ly soft on her himself. Anyway, I think he might be prepared to get a message to Becky if'n I can come up with some sort'a plan, an' she's not too scared to co-operate.' He remembered her frightened face as she walked away from the funeral.

'You be careful, son,' Smokey said. 'They're a treacherous bunch. None of 'em can be trusted, includin' the kid, an' you could find yourself walkin' into a trap.'

'Might have to take that chance,' Tom said.

He finished his meal and walked across the street to the hotel. The desk clerk looked up as he came in. He peered across the top of his eyeglasses at Tom.

'You need your key?' he asked.

'Not just yet,' Tom said. 'I need some information. You've got a man called Garrod stayin' here, that right?'

The clerk frowned. 'I don't think so.'

'About fifty,' Tom said. 'Fat, with greyin' hair. Always wears a suit with a frock coat.'

'Oh, you mean Mr Granger,' the clerk said. 'Yes, he's staying here. At least, he was. He booked in yesterday morning, but as far as I know, nobody's seen him since. Asked for a room with two beds, like he was expectin' to meet up with somebody who'd be staying with him.'

'That right?' Tom said. He thought for a moment. 'Any chance I could look into his room? He's a friend of mine,' he added, seeing the other man hesitate. 'I'm kind'a worried about him.'

'A friend, but you didn't know his name?' the clerk said, suspiciously.

Tom smiled. 'Seems he uses a different name some-times.' He flicked the silver star on his waistcoat, as if to make a point. 'Now, about that room.'

The clerk sighed. 'I guess it'll be all right, you being a lawman.' He turned and took a key from one of the hooks behind him. 'Room five,' he said.

Tom took the key and walked along the passage, check-ing the doors. Room five was at the end. He used the key to go inside.

The room boasted two single beds, a washstand, and a rail along one wall. A black slicker hung from the rail, and there was a leather bag beside the bed. Tom opened it and looked inside. A change of underwear, nothing else. No indication of why he had come to Weslake, although Tom was pretty sure he knew why – to somehow negotiate for the release of his daughter. *Or maybe to collect her as due payment for aiding the raid on the Solace bank?* So why hadn't he returned to the hotel? Suddenly, Tom had a bad feeling.

It would soon be time to meet up with Clay Thornton or Chet Adams or whatever his name was, and see if they could work out a plan to get Becky Garrod out of Eli Pike's clutches. Something, Tom was beginning to think, Harvey Garrod had failed to do. Meantime, he'd go back to the

127

café and ponder over a pot of coffee until it got dark. He had to come up with a plan.

CHAPTER
TWENTY-TWO

Just before nine o'clock, from his vantage point amongst the dark shadows of the boardwalk outside the Weslake apothecary, Nate Morgan watched the Solace deputy leave the café and cross the street towards the hotel. Nate debated whether or not to gun the youngster down immediately, or go into the hotel and finish him off there.

Nate had no fears about the hotel clerk obstructing him. Like a lot of other people in Weslake, the man was in the pay of Eli Pike.

He decided to wait a while and see what happened.

In the event, the young man went past the main door of the hotel and, after glancing around, disappeared up the passageway at the side of the building.

'So where's he goin'?' Nate muttered to himself.

As far as he knew, the passageway led only to the rear of the hotel and a walled yard. Was the lawman meeting someone? If he was, judging by the deputy's furtive manner, it was a meeting that either he or the other person wanted to keep confidential.

Again, Nate decided to wait and see what developed.

And again, he didn't have to wait long. Minutes later he saw a familiar figure enter the passageway in a similarly covert manner.

The kid!

Now why was Chet Adams meeting up with the deputy? None of the answers Nate could come up with pleased him. There could only be one reason – a double-cross of some sort. Some kind of bargain to be struck? Some deal that would get the kid off the hook from the law in exchange for informing on Eli?

'Reckon there'll have to be two killin's 'stead of one,' Nate muttered to himself. He smiled at the prospect.

He drifted out from the shadows, pulling down the rim of his hat to conceal his face, and headed towards the hotel, leading his horse. After tethering the piebald to the hitching rail at the front of the building, he moved across to the passageway.

The only light in the yard behind the hotel came from one of the back rooms and, intermittently, the moon as clouds opened to reveal its face. Tom heard the footsteps in the passageway and guessed it was the kid. Even so, he was taking no chances and eased his .45 from its holster and stepped back into the shadows.

'Walsh?' Clay Thornton's voice was a whisper.

Tom stepped out into the light, but only after he had checked that the other man wasn't wielding a weapon. 'Over here.'

The two men drew closer to each other.

130

'Eli would kill me if he knew I was talkin' to you,' Clay said.

'So we won't tell him,' Tom said.

'An' I ain't sure how I can help you.'

'Me neither, just yet,' Tom said.

'So how're you plannin' on getting Becky away from Pike?' Clay asked. 'Like I said, Eli keeps her pretty close most of the time. An' he's even more likely to do that now he knows you're in town.'

'Becky's pa was in town earlier an' he ain't reappeared,' Tom said. 'Know anythin' about that?'

Clay hesitated for a moment, then said, 'Garrod's dead.'

Tom sighed. 'I'd kind'a figured that. You can explain how that happened later. First tell me about the Solace bank raid. What happened there? Why was it necessary to gun down the teller an' the manager? An' which one of those two killed Eli Pike's brother Silas?'

Clay shook his head. 'I ain't talkin' about the raid,' he said. 'That ain't why I'm here. If'n you want to nail Eli for the robbery, you're gonna have to do it without my help.'

'Somethin' went wrong, didn't it?' Tom persisted. 'There wasn't meant to be any killin', that's my bet.'

Clay made no reply.

'OK, have it your way,' Tom said after a moment or two. 'Let's figure out how we're going to rescue Becky Garrod from that scumbag's clutches. First thing you've got to do is let her know I'm gonna help her. Then . . .'

He broke off suddenly.

'What is it?' Clay whispered, suddenly tense.

Tom put a finger to his lips and withdrew his .45 from

his holster. Clay saw him and replicated the action. Both men shifted into the shadow of the hotel's back wall, their eyes on the end of the passageway, watching for movement.

'*You there, Chet?*' The rasping voice came out of the blackness.

'Nate Morgan,' Clay said, and even in the semi-darkness, Tom saw the kid's face blanch at the sound of the outlaw's menacing utterance.

'OK, listen to me kid,' Morgan continued. 'Whatever it was you were plannin' with the lawman, it ain't gonna happen, you hear that? He's a dead man, you can rely on it. So you've got a choice. Die alongside him, or use your gun on him. You've got thirty seconds to decide.'

It was the longest speech Clay had ever heard Nate Morgan make, but as he wavered over his decision, he saw that Tom Walsh's gun had moved and was now aiming directly at him.

'His choice is made, Morgan,' Tom called to the other man. 'He's in no position to kill me, not whilst I'm coverin' him with my .45.'

Silence.

'It's make-your-mind-up time, kid.' Tom pulled the youngster deeper into the shadows. 'You're either with me, or you're with Morgan. Although I wouldn't give a plugged nickel for your chances with Morgan now, whatever happens, so make your mind up fast.'

Clay looked like a trapped animal as he pondered. He swallowed. 'I . . . I guess I'm with you.'

At the same moment there was a burst of sound as Morgan threw himself out of the passageway in a roll, firing in the direction of Tom's voice. His broad-brimmed hat skittered across the yard.

Tom felt a burning sensation in his arm as one of Nate's bullets winged him. Even so, he pushed Clay to the ground and threw himself after him, rolling over and returning a rattle of shots, aiming at the orange flame from Morgan's gun.

He was rewarded with the sound of an agonized grunt and the clatter of a dropped firearm.

Silence.

'Morgan?' Tom yelled.

At that moment, the clouds parted and a shaft of moonlight revealed the slumped form of Nate Morgan, his sightless eyes staring into the sky, blood seeping from wounds in his neck and chest and from the corners of his mouth.

Tom let out a long breath, then turned his attention to his companion, holstering his six-shooter. 'Seems you made the right decision, kid,' he said. He used his free hand and his teeth to tie his neckerchief around the wound on his arm, wincing with pain. The youngster made no move to help him. 'You reckon?'

Clay Thornton holstered his own .45. 'I guess it does,' he said.

Tom wiped the sweat from his forehead with the back of his hand and gritted his teeth against the pain in his arm. 'To my reckonin', that only leaves Eli Pike to contend with. Am I right?'

Clay nodded. 'Yeah, you are. But there's still Becky to get away safely. How're you gonna do that, 'specially now you're injured?'

133

Tom tried to arrange his thoughts. Then he spotted Nate Morgan's hat, resting on its crown near the outlaw's body, and an idea began to form in his mind. 'OK, first I'm gonna go find the local doc to fix my arm,' he said. 'Then . . .'

The sound of approaching footsteps stopped him. Moments later, Cord Lewis and two other figures emerged hesitantly from the passageway. Tom recognized Smokey Harrison as one of them, but not the bearded man beside the old-timer. The three of them took in the scene, then the sheriff swore and ran his hand over his face.

'Jeeze, is that who I think it is,' he said, looking at Morgan's body.

The bearded man moved swiftly across to the recumbent form. 'Don't need me to tell you he's dead, Cord,' he said, after a moment. 'There's nothing I can do for him.' He glanced across at Tom and took in the bloodstained neckerchief. 'I'm a doctor, and it looks like I need to tend to your arm, mister.'

Tom nodded. 'Yeah, thanks.'

'Not 'til I've finished with him, you ain't, Doc,' the sheriff growled. 'I wanna know what's been happenin' here.'

'Looks pretty damn obvious to me, Cord,' Smokey Harrison put in, a twinkle in his eye. 'Seems like our friend here has done us the favour of puttin' one more of Pike's henchmen out of action. Town'll be that much safer without that varmint.'

Cord turned his attention to Clay. 'What's your part in all this, kid? Looks to me like you've changed sides all of a damn sudden!'

Clay stared back without speaking.

Cord shrugged. 'OK, have it your way. Smokey, you go fetch Abe Lucre to see to the body, an' . . .'

'Hang on, sheriff,' Tom said. 'I've got plans for Morgan, soon as the doc here has fixed my arm.'

'Plans?'

'Thought I might let Eli Pike decide what to do with Morgan's body,' Tom said.

'You mean you're plannin' to take him to the Lazy O?'

'Yeah, that's right,' Tom said. 'You got any objection?'

'Are you crazy?' Cord sighed. 'Oh, hell! Do what you damn well please. Eli's gonna blame me anyways. Reckon I'm finished in this damn town! Time I moved on.'

And with that, he turned and walked away.

'Reckon it is, Cord,' Smokey said, to the sheriff's retreating back. 'An' that ain't no bad thing, either. What d'you say, Doc?'

'I say this young deputy's got a whole heap of trouble coming to him if he goes to the Lazy O with Nate Morgan's body draped over his horse.' The medical man looked at Clay. 'You planning to go with him, kid?'

Tom and Clay exchanged glances.

'Yeah, I guess I'm going with him,' Clay said. 'He's gonna need me to get anywhere near the ranch house, once Eli's seen Nate's body.'

'Matter of fact,' Tom said. 'You'll be goin' on ahead of me, kid.'

'I will?' Clay said.

Tom nodded. 'You've got a story to tell afore I put in an appearance at the ranch. I just hope you can be convincin', 'cause I reckon Becky's life may depend on it.'

Smokey smiled. 'Seems like this here lawman's got a plan, Doc,' he said.

'I just need a few directions to get me to the ranch,' Tom said.

Smokey grinned. 'No problem there, son.'

CHAPTER TWENTY-THREE

Becky watched as Eli paced up and down the room of the ranch house, chewing on a cheroot and cursing savagely under his breath. She had never seen him like this, so distracted and ill at ease. But then, he had never before lost two of his men in such quick succession. It didn't bode well for her later, when he became less preoccupied.

The loot from the bank raid still lay in the saddle-bags and bulging canvas moneybags on the large oak desk in the corner. This in itself was a sure sign Eli had more important things on his mind than bedding Becky.

For the past hour she had tried to keep herself as inconspicuous as possible, and for once, he seemed almost totally unaware of her presence. Which was just as well, as she was still numb from the news of her father's death. Every time she thought of it a sharp pain seemed to gnaw at her insides and tears threatened to spring from her eyes.

What had really happened at Checker Pass? Not for a minute did she believe the story Eli had told her – that her father had pulled a gun on Chet and Ray, and that the latter had shot her pa in self-defence. Although she supposed it was just possible a lucky stray bullet from her pa's gun had killed Ray Riggens. Unfortunately there had been no opportunity since then for her to get Chet alone and extract the true story from him.

Where he was at this moment, she had no idea. Still in Weslake? Eli clearly expected him to return sometime soon. A thought struck her that set her heart palpitating. Was it possible Chet had somehow managed to make a break? That he *wasn't coming back?* She could hardly blame him, even though he had given her the impression that, if he did make a break for it, he would take her with him.

Nor, for that matter, could she guess where Nate had got to. The only thing she could be sure of was that, wherever he was and whatever instructions Eli may have given him, it wouldn't bode well for Tom Walsh, the young deputy from Solace.

Becky had been shocked to see him at Silas' funeral. Momentarily her spirits had risen. Would *he* be able to help her? Could *he* get her away from this place? But as soon as she considered the odds, she discounted the possibility. They were all in Eli's favour, she decided. Even allowing for Chet's feelings for her and his desire to help her, there was always Nate Morgan. He did Eli's every bidding and would kill Chet without question. That had been her thoughts after the funeral. But now. . . .

Abruptly, Eli ceased his pacing and moved towards the door. Becky listened, and heard the sound of an approaching rider.

Just the one.

Nate? Was it a case of 'job done'? Was Tom Walsh dead?

She followed Eli out on to the porch, keeping into the background. After a minute her eyes adjusted to the darkness and she was able to discern the identity of the rider – and heaved a sigh of relief.

It was Chet. At least he was still alive.

She watched the young man dismount slowly as Eli hurried from the porch to meet him.

'Where'n hell've you been?' Eli snarled.

'In town,' Clay replied. 'I was . . . er . . . enjoyin' the delights of Maisie in her room at the Holed Ace. Got kinda carried away an' stayed longer than I'd planned.'

'Have you seen Nate?'

Clay nodded. 'I was about to tell you. I saw him as I was comin' out of the saloon. He told me that you'd told him to get rid of that deputy.'

'So what happened?' Eli towered over the youngster. 'Is Nate all right? Spit it out, for chris'sakes!'

'Yeah, he's fine. Well, 'cept for a flesh wound which he's gettin' fixed by the doc right now.'

'Flesh wound? What about the lawman from Solace? Nate was supposed to deal with him without anyone knowin' it was him.'

'Things didn't quite work out like that,' Clay said. 'The lawman's dead all right. Stretched out in an alleyway at the side of the hotel, last I saw. But he managed to get off the shot that winged Nate before Nate plugged him.'

As Becky heard this she gave a gasp and put a hand to her mouth. Tom Walsh was dead! Poor Meg Thornton, she thought, for once harbouring no jealous thoughts against the young woman. There would be no wedding now.

She watched the tension drain from Eli's body as he received the news. 'Good,' he said after a moment. 'When does Nate reckon he'll be back?'

'Within the next hour, I'd guess,' Clay said. 'His wound was nothin' much. The doc'll fix it in no time.' He made a great show of rubbing his forehead and staggering slightly on his feet. 'Jeeze, Eli, I need to lie down. What with Maisie's enthusiastic lovin' an' that gutrot whiskey they serve in the Holed Ace, I'm jiggered.'

Eli looked him up and down. 'Get yourself off to the bunkhouse, kid,' he told him. 'I'll send Becky across with some coffee.'

'Yeah, thanks Eli,' Clay said. 'I could sure use some.' And he led his horse away.

Eli turned to Becky. 'You heard what I said. Get the kid some coffee.'

'Sure, Eli,' Becky said.

At about the same time Clay was heading towards the bunkhouse, Floyd Wickes rode into Weslake. His first port of call was the local sheriff's office.

Cord Lewis was sleeping on the bunk in an open cell, snoring and grunting spasmodically. With a look of distaste, Floyd moved into the cell and shook the other man's shoulder.

'Whaaat! Jeeze, I . . .' Cord blinked and peered at the figure standing over him. 'Who in hell are you?' he growled.

'Floyd Wickes. Sheriff of Solace,' Floyd informed him.

'Jeeze, another damn lawman from that town!' Cord said. His head felt as though he'd been kicked by a mule,

140

and he was having trouble straightening his thoughts.

'So you've met my deputy,' Floyd said.

'Damn right I have,' Cord said, heaving himself from the bunk and standing unsteadily. 'Caused a whole heap of trouble since he hit town.'

'So maybe you'll tell me where I can find him,' Floyd said.

'Well, I won't,' Cord told him. 'He ain't my responsibility when he goes pokin' his nose into other people's. . . .' his voice trailed away as he realized he was recklessly shooting his mouth off.

Floyd nodded. 'By that you mean he was askin' about the Pike gang.'

'I ain't sayin' nothin',' Cord said.

'That figures,' Floyd said. 'I reckoned Eli Pike would need an accommodatin' sheriff. One who'd look the other way when necessary.'

'Now listen here. . . !' Cord began.

Floyd waved his protest away. 'Forget it. Guess I'll just have to ask around, startin' with the saloon, then maybe the hotel.'

Fifteen minutes later, having found Smokey Harrison telling anyone who'd listen about the demise of Morgan, and the intentions of 'that crazy deputy from Solace', Floyd headed out of town in a hurry.

'Watch out for yourself!' Smokey called after him. 'You an' that kid are about to start tanglin' with a rattlesnake!'

CHAPTER TWENTY-FOUR

Clay was sitting on the edge of his bunk when Becky arrived with a pot of coffee and a mug.

'I was sure worried about you, Chet.' She was surprised to see him looking so alert after the way he'd acted outside. Now he spoke briskly and it took her no more than a moment to realize he'd been play-acting earlier.

'Help's comin', Becky,' he said.

'Help?' She looked startled.

'Any luck, an' we'll both be out'a here afore sun-up,' Clay said.

'How d'you mean?' She poured some coffee into the mug and handed it to him, her hand shaking with excitement.

Clay gulped it down. 'Where's Eli?'

'Sittin' with a bottle of bourbon, waitin' for Nate to come back,' she said.

'He'll have a long wait. Nate ain't comin' back,' Clay told her. 'He's dead.'

'But you told Eli . . .'

'Yeah, I know what I told him. It was all lies. Tom Walsh killed Nate. It's Walsh who's gettin' his arm fixed by the doc, not Nate. It's Walsh who'll be here within the hour.'

'What's he going to do?' Becky's head was in a whirl.

'He plans to take Eli back to Solace to face a trial, usin' me as a witness to Eli's killin' of the bank manager.'

Becky stared at him in astonishment, trying to take it all in. 'But . . . but what about you? Even though you didn't kill anybody, you were part of the robbery. Won't that mean prison?'

'Prob'ly,' Clay said. *As long as Meg keeps her mouth shut about who really killed the teller – me, not Silas.* 'That ain't decided. Walsh says the law'll go easy on me if'n I give testimony against Eli. Maybe just a short spell in Yuma prison.' Clay gave a short mirthless chuckle. ' 'Ceptin' I don't plan to hang around to find out, once I know you're safe. If the law wants me, it'll have to come after me.' He looked at Becky. 'An' Walsh may not want to do that after he hears what you're gonna tell him.'

Becky frowned. 'Yeah? What am I going to tell him?'

'That Meg Thornton, the girl he's plannin' to marry, is my sister,' Clay said. 'That'll probl'y give him pause for thought.'

'Your *sister*?' She stared at him. 'But your name's Adams . . . ain't it?'

Clay shook his head. 'It's Thornton. *Clay* Thornton.' He saw the stunned look on her face and forestalled her string of questions with, 'It's a long story, Becky. Get Meg to tell it to you sometime. An' get her to tell you an' Walsh what really happened at the bank raid in Solace. By then

I'll be long gone, to somewhere safe, if I'm lucky. An' I plan to be.'

She stared at him, her head in a spin. 'But how is Tom Walsh going to ride into the ranch without Eli seeing him?'

Clay smiled. 'Eli *will* see him. Only it'll be "Nate" he sees.'

Becky looked confused. 'I don't understand.'

'Don't worry about it. Just get some things together an' be ready to leave. I'm gonna saddle a coupl'a horses as soon as you've gone back to the house, so keep Eli away from the window.'

'This is crazy,' she said. 'We'll never get away with . . .'

He put a hand on her arm. 'It's gonna be OK. Trust me.'

Eli was sitting at the pine table, morosely nursing a tumbler of bourbon. The strain of the last few days was showing on his face. Not only had he lost his brother, but he'd lost Ray Riggins, one of his best gunman. And Ray, being the oldest, had been a calming influence when things went wrong. Eli knew he'd miss him.

His gunbelt, with both holsters holding a six-gun, was slung over the back of the chair next to him. An oil lamp burned in the centre of the table. He looked up as Becky returned clutching the coffee pot.

'You were a long time,' he said, suspiciously. 'What were you doin'?'

'I . . . I waited to bring back the coffee,' she said. 'Do you want some?'

He shook his head. 'You weren't cosyin' up to the kid,

144

were you?' he said, eyeing her carefully.

' 'Course not.'

Becky could feel her heart thumping in her breast.

'You know he's soft on you, don't you?'

She gave a nervous little laugh. 'Don't be silly, Eli,' she said.

'Believe me, the horny little bastard would be only too happy to get you between the sheets if'n I gave him half a chance,' Eli said. 'Ain't you seen the way he looks at you?'

Becky blushed. 'He won't do anythin'.'

'Damn right, he won't!' Eli said, belligerently. 'You're my property, girl, an' don't you forget it!' His voice softened slightly as he went on. ''Sides, now your pa's dead, you're gonna need somebody to look out for you.' He shook his head. 'Don't know what got into him, tryin' to gun down Ray an' Chet. It was a stupid thing to do, Becky, you know that, don't you?'

'Sure, Eli,' Becky said, quietly. She faked a yawn. 'I . . . I guess I'll go to bed now, if that's OK. I'm real tuckered out.'

'Yeah, that's OK.' He swallowed a mouthful of bourbon. 'You go on up. I'm gonna wait for Nate, hear what happened from him. Reckon the kid only had half the story.' He glanced up at her. 'We'll prob'ly move on from here tomorrow,' he said.

'We will?'

'Yeah. Kinda outstayed our welcome in Weslake, I'm reckonin'. Not sure if Nate'll want to come along with us, you can never tell what he's thinkin'. Keeps his cards close to his chest. Anyways, I'll leave it to him. But you take yourself off to bed an' get some sleep.' He gave a sly grin. 'I

might decide to wake you up for a bit of lovin' later. OK?'
He laughed and poured himself another shot of bourbon.

'Uh . . . OK.' Becky gave a half-smile. Then she remembered what Chet . . . Clay had told her about Tom Walsh coming soon, and a feeling of relief swept over her as she escaped to her room.

CHAPTER
TWENTY-FIVE

Clad in Nate Morgan's long riding duster and with the brim of Morgan's broad-brimmed hat pulled low over his forehead, Tom rode the piebald gelding towards the ranch house at a steady trot. Behind him, he trailed his own horse with Morgan's body slung over the saddle. Just how near he would get before Eli Pike realized he wasn't Morgan, Tom couldn't be sure. It was a gamble, but a gamble worth taking if it meant getting Becky Garrod out of Pike's clutches. And at least the makeshift 'disguise' gave him a chance to get close enough to spring his surprise and draw Morgan's Winchester from the saddle boot.

The arm that Nate's bullet had winged was bandaged under the duster and gave off a dull ache, but the doc in Weslake had done a good job of patching him up. Good enough for what he had to do now, at any rate.

'Best of luck, young'un,' Smokey Harrison had said to him, after helping to tie down Nate's body on Tom's horse.

147

'Reckon you're gonna need it.'

It seemed that the old-timer, like others in that town, had a vested interest in seeing Eli Pike brought to justice, driven out of the territory – or better still, killed.

Tom looked across at the ranch house. He could see the light from the living-room oil lamp and the silhouetted form of Eli as the latter, hearing Tom's approach, rose from his chair. The only other light in the building was upstairs, and Tom hoped this meant that Becky Garrod was preparing to leave – if necessary, in a hurry. That Clay Thornton had forewarned her.

Eli emerged from the house on to the porch above the step. Tom noted he was not wearing his gunbelt. 'Nate?' he called. 'You OK?'

Tom made no reply, just kept riding. Casually, he let his hand drift down to the stock of the Winchester and closed his fingers around it.

'Heard you got a bullet,' Eli said. 'The doc fix you up OK? Only I. . . .' He stopped abruptly. 'Sonofabitch! You ain't . . .' The words trailed off as he saw Tom draw the Winchester from its scabbard. A slow smile spread across his face. 'The lawman from Solace! Well, I'll be damned.'

Tom nodded. 'More'n likely you will.'

Eli gave a rueful grin. 'Well, I guess you bein' here means Nate's gone to meet his maker. That his body you're towin' behind you?'

'That's right, Eli,' Tom said, reining the piebald to a halt a few feet from the porch and levelling the rifle so that it pointed directly at Eli's chest.

Out of the corner of his eye he saw Clay Thornton leading two saddled horses from the corral, his six-gun drawn in readiness for trouble.

Eli noticed him, too, and sighed. 'So the kid was lyin',' he said. He glanced at Clay. 'The lawman talk you round to takin' his side, Chet?'

Clay halted the two horses alongside the piebald. 'Guess he did, Eli,' he answered. 'Didn't take much persuadin', not after the way you've been treatin' Becky.'

Eli nodded. 'Thought as much. It's like I was just tellin' her, you're soft on her, ain't you? Well, it makes no nevermind 'cause she ain't goin' anywhere. She's stayin' with me.'

'Untie Morgan's body,' Tom told Clay without taking his eyes off Eli. 'I want to be ridin' my own horse when we leave here.'

Clay did as he was asked, and Tom heard the *thrump* as Morgan's corpse hit the dirt.

'Now go fetch Becky from inside the house, kid,' Tom said.

'N . . . no need to!' The unsteady voice came from the ranch-house doorway, where Becky was standing a few feet behind Eli. 'I'm here.' She was holding a carpetbag and was wearing jeans, a shirt and a tooled leather vest.

Eli turned and looked at her. 'Ready to travel?' he said, the sneer in his voice only too apparent. 'Shame you won't be goin' anyplace, leastways not with these critters.'

'We're all goin', you included, Pike,' Tom said. 'We're goin' back to Solace, where you'll spend some time in Sheriff Wickes's jail afore bein' tried by the circuit judge. Then you'll be hanged for the murder of Arthur Makin, the bank manager.'

Eli laughed. 'That so?' He looked at Clay. 'An' what

about you, kid? What's this here deputy told you? That the judge'll go easy on you after you give testimony against me? Well, good luck with that kid, but I wouldn't count on it. Believe me, it'll make more sense if'n you gun down this lawman an' come back an' join me an' Becky.'

'So you could kill me?' Clay shouted. 'No deal, Eli. An' Becky's comin' with us.'

'Listen, you want Becky?' Eli said. 'OK, you can have her. I'm kinda bored with her, anyways. Jus' come with me.'

In the course of this conversation, Tom had dismounted the piebald whilst Clay kept Eli covered with his six-gun.

'We was plannin' on leavin' here tomorrow anyways, ain't that right, girl?' Eli went on. 'Gettin' away from Weslake. The three of us could start up again someplace else, kid.'

'He's lyin', Clay,' Tom said, gathering up the reins of his horse.

' "Clay"?' What's with this "Clay"? That your real name, kid? Well, well, the night's full of surprises. Not that it matters none. You'll still be better off with me, kid. 'Sides, you ain't had your share of the money from the bank raid,' Eli persisted, seeing Clay wavering. 'With jus' the two of us left, that's more'n ten thousand dollars apiece. You gonna pass up ten thousand dollars an' take your chances on avoidin' spendin' the next ten years in jail, kid?'

Clay's thoughts whirled. Doubts began to seep into the edges of his mind. *Ten thousand dollars!* He could start a whole new life with that amount of money. And maybe there would still be an opportunity to get away with Becky,

150

once he'd got his share.

And Yuma prison beckoned if he hooked up with the lawman.

Tom saw that the kid was wavering. 'Don't listen to him, Clay,' he said, gathering up the reins of his horse. 'He's . . .'

But Clay had made up his mind. '*Change of plan, lawman!*' he said.

CHAPTER TWENTY-SIX

He wheeled and pointed his .45 at Tom. 'Eli's right, there ain't no guarantee I won't end up in Yuma, doin' a ten-stretch.'

'Now you're seein' sense, kid,' Eli said.

'Drop the Winchester an' undo your gunbelt!' Clay told Tom.

Tom sighed, dropped the rifle and released his gunbelt so that it fell to the dirt. 'You're a fool, Thornton, if you think you'll live to see any of that money,' he said. 'Pike'll gun you down soon as he gets his hand on a weapon. An' what about Becky? You gonna leave her at the mercy of that evil critter?'

'Shut up!' Clay said. 'Just get on your horse an' ride out.'

'No, you can't let him do that, kid!' Eli yelled. 'You're gonna have to kill him!'

Clay glanced over his shoulder at Eli, then back again at Tom, as he vacillated.

'He's right, Clay,' Tom said, calmly. 'You're gonna have to kill me. You up to that?' He could see the beads of sweat on the young man's forehead, in spite of the coolness of the night.

'Do it, kid!' The impatience in Eli's voice was clear. 'Plug him! It ain't as though it'll be your first. You killed the bank teller, remember?'

'I . . . I can't,' Clay said, eventually.

'Why?' Eli demanded. 'What's so different about this *hombre*?'

'*He's going to marry Clay's sister, that's what's different about him!*' screamed Becky, suddenly finding her voice. 'Clay, you can't kill your sister's fiancé!'

Eli turned and peered at Becky. 'What in hell are you talkin' about?'

She looked back, not answering.

'You're . . . you're Meg's brother?' Tom said, staring at Clay.

Clay nodded. 'Yeah, I am.' He steadied his gun hand. 'So get on your horse an' ride, afore I change my mind!'

'No!' Eli shouted. 'If you won't kill him, let me, kid. This ain't no time for sentiment. He's a lawman, an' even if you let him go, he'll jus' hunt you down again. Ain't that right, lawman?'

'Yep, I guess it is,' Tom said, looking straight at Clay. ' 'Specially now I know it was you who killed Howie Clark. Howie was a good friend of mine.'

'I . . . I had to,' Clay said. 'Or he would've shot me.'

'Throw me his six-gun, kid,' Eli yelled. 'I'll finish him, you don't have to do anythin'. Jus' come an' look after Becky.'

Clay glanced back at him, then bent down and scooped up Tom's Peacemaker. He was about to toss it back to Eli when a voice came from somewhere behind Tom.

'*Hold everythin*!'

It was followed by a rifle shot that echoed in the stillness and kicked up splinters from the porch floor at Eli's feet.

'Sheeit!' Eli swore as the figure emerged from the shadows.

'*Floyd?*' Tom said, recognizing the voice. 'Hell, am I glad to see you!'

He snatched his six-gun from the dithering Clay's grasp and used the barrel to knock the youngster's own gun from his hand. Then he snatched up the discarded Winchester and ran to Floyd's side.

'You OK, Tom?' Floyd asked.

'I am now you're here,' Tom answered. 'What brought you?'

'The truth about what happened at the bank,' Floyd answered. 'I'll tell it to you later. It's some story.'

'I think I'm beginnin' to find out some of it anyways,' Tom said, staring at Clay.

'OK, but right now we need to attend to these two varmints,' Floyd said.

During this exchange, unnoticed by either of them, Eli had imperceptibly inched his way back towards Becky. Equally, the girl had been too busy watching Tom and Floyd to notice Eli's movements, so that when he sprang, it took her completely by surprise.

He threw himself against her, his weight pushing her back into the house before he kicked the door shut behind them. Becky screamed as they crashed to the

154

floor in a heap, Eli's body knocking the breath from her chest.

The belated shot from Floyd's Winchester splintered the doorframe but was otherwise ineffective. He cursed and spurred his horse away from the line of the door. The remaining horses scattered as Tom ran for cover.

Clay whirled from side to side, then made for the house. 'I'm comin' in, Eli!' he yelled. 'Don't shoot!'

Floyd lifted his rifle and aimed at Clay's retreating form.

'No!' Tom shouted. 'Leave him, Floyd. He's Meg's brother!'

'He's still a killer,' Floyd yelled, but withheld his fire.

'Just take cover! Pike's gonna start shootin' any minute!'

Inside the house, Eli had been quick to get to his feet, dragging Becky up by her arm and throwing her into a corner of the room. 'Stay there, bitch!' he'd snarled, then snatched his gunbelt from the back of the chair. He shoved the table up against the door to act as a barricade, then crouched and made his way to the window. He smashed the glass with the barrel of his .45 and fired a warning shot into the darkness. 'Stay back lawmen!' he yelled. 'Or I kill the girl!'

Becky was making noises like a small animal in the corner, curled up in a foetal position, still clutching her carpetbag. She heard Clay hammering on the blocked door.

'Eli! Let me in afore they kill me!'

For a reply, Eli poked his gun out of the holed glass and

fired a single sideways shot. There was the sound of a scream, then of Clay falling on to the boards – then nothing.

Floyd was at one end of the porch, flattened against the corner of the ranch house, the Winchester in his hand. He could see Tom prone on the ground, below the step, clutching his .45. The younger man had swiftly discarded Nate Morgan's riding duster and hat so he could move more easily. They lay in a heap in the dirt a few feet from him, like the ghost of the dead outlaw.

Both lawmen had ducked instinctively as Eli smashed the window and fired the warning shot into the darkness. Both now heard the second shot and saw Clay Thornton collapse and lie still, half his face blown away.

Floyd dropped to his hands and knees and crab-walked along the porch and under the window until he reached the door. Avoiding Clay's body, he heaved his shoulder against the door, testing it for an obstruction, and wasn't surprised when it didn't budge.

Eli's voice came from the window. 'Listen up, out there! You want this girl to live, you're gonna do as I tell you. Hear me?'

Tom waited a few moments, then said, 'We hear you, Pike.'

'OK. Now you're both gonna toss your six-guns an' rifles next to the kid. Then you're gonna walk slowly, hands in the air, an' get the two saddled horses Clay brought out earlier. You're gonna bring 'em to the porch an' leave 'em by the steps. You got that?'

'Sure, Pike,' Tom said. 'Just don't hurt the girl.'

'Next you're gonna back away an' lie down flat on the ground until Becky an' me have ridden out of here,' Eli said. 'Try anythin' fancy, an' the girl dies. Got that?'

'We got it, Pike,' Floyd said, nodding at Tom to reciprocate.

'Yeah, we got it,' Tom said.

Both men threw their weapons on to the porch so that they landed either side of Clay Thornton's body. Then, careful to keep out of the line of fire, they backed off towards the corral, near to which the spooked creatures had scampered at the sound of the shooting.

Floyd and Tom each caught one of the two saddled horses and walked them slowly across to the house.

'You know he's gonna kill the pair of us as soon as he walks out'a that door, don't you?' Tom whispered.

Floyd nodded. 'I know. Got any ideas?'

'Just the one,' Tom told him. 'Not sure if it's gonna work though. I used to be pretty good at it when I was a kid, but I'm kind'a out'a practice these days.'

'At what?' Floyd said.

'You'll see,' Tom said. Then added with a grin, 'Unless you're dead first.'

Eli watched as the two men walked the horses across to the railing around the porch, keeping the animals between themselves and Eli's line of fire. He waited until both horses were loosely tethered over the rail.

'Now back away!' he yelled. 'Slowly.'

Tom and Floyd complied.

'Lie down on the ground!' Eli yelled through the window, then cursed as the moon went behind a large bank of cloud.

When he could just about see through the darkness that they'd done as he'd ordered, he crossed the room and yanked Becky to her feet. 'Let's go,' he told her.

Sobbing, Becky allowed herself to be dragged across to the door, where Eli kicked away the obstruction, then shoved her out on to the porch. He checked the two men were lying on the ground, both face down, then he pushed Becky towards one of the horses.

'Mount up,' he told her. 'An' don't do anythin' stupid lessen you want a bullet through that pretty head of yours. You hear?'

'Sure, Eli,' Becky answered. 'I . . . I hear.'

He waited for her to get on the horse, then walked across to the two prone lawmen.

'Gonna shoot us in the back, Pike?' Tom taunted. 'Guess that's the way you're used to killin' men.'

Eli snickered. 'Feelin' brave, mister? You wanna look me in the eye when you die? Suits me. Turn over, lawman!'

It was a fatal error.

Tom turned fast, his right hand coming from under his body – and Eli saw the glint of something long and sharp just before it hit him in the chest. He gasped and staggered, a look of astonishment, then pain spreading across his face. Somehow he managed to pull the trigger on his six-gun, but by that time, both lawmen had rolled sideways so that his bullet hit the dirt harmlessly.

Eli sensed a swift movement as he tumbled forwards, his face creased in agony, then felt the .45 snatched from his grasp. He fell on to the knife, thrusting it deeper into his chest until the blade snapped from the handle.

He didn't get up. A smattering of weak, indecipherable

curses came from his mouth, along with a stream of blood, before he fell silent.

The two lawmen looked down on him.

'Guess he's cheated the hangman,' Floyd said, grimacing.

'Guess so,' Tom agreed.

Becky ran across to him and threw herself into the sheriff's arms, making him wince.

'There, there, it's OK,' Floyd told her, holding her close. 'Everythin's gonna be fine.' He looked across at Tom. 'Ain't never seen you carryin' a knife afore. Didn't know you were handy with 'em, either.'

'It was Morgan's,' Tom explained, grinning. 'Found it in a sheath in his boot. Clay told me he always kept one there. I borrowed it, along with his coat an' hat, an' his horse. As to bein' handy with knives, I used to be able to hit a playin' card from twenty feet when I was a kid. Got kind'a rusty of late, though, so it was just as well Pike was leanin' over me, otherwise I could've missed.'

'Sure happy you didn't,' Floyd said, smiling.

Becky had eased herself from Floyd's arms and was looking at the body on the porch. 'Wh . . . what are you going to tell Meg about her brother, Tom?'

'The truth, I guess,' he said. 'That's usually the best way.' He looked at Floyd. 'You were goin' to tell me what really happened at the bank raid with Meg's brother. Seems there's a few more things I don't know.'

'Reckon I'll let Meg tell you,' Floyd said. 'It ain't somethin' she's been proud of keepin' from you.'

Tom shrugged. 'It ain't gonna change the way I feel about her,' he said.

Floyd and Becky exchanged a conspiratorial look. 'That's love for you,' Floyd said.

'Reckon it is,' she agreed.